AMISH II
(6 BOOK BOXSET)
AMISH MYSTERY AND ROMANCE

Rachel H. Kester

Clean Stories Publishing

Copyright 2016 © Rachel H. Kester

All right reserved

This is a work of fiction. Names, characters, businesses, places, events and incidents are either the products of the author's imagination or used in a fictitious manner. Any resemblance to actual persons, living or dead, or actual events is purely coincidental.

Amish Investigation

Amish Investigation

TABLE OF CONTENT

Table of Content 3

THE PLAIN ART OF MURDER 8

    Chapter 1 - A Gut Day Gone Bad 9

    Chapter 2 - Crime Scene 15

    Chapter 3 - Accused 21

    Chapter 4 - Too Many Questions, Not Enough Answers 28

    Chapter 5 - Clueless 33

    Chapter 6 - Another Dead End 38

    Chapter 7 - And Then There Were Two 45

    Chapter 8 - Dark Days 51

    Chapter 9 - A Last Goodbye 57

    Chapter 10 - Gut's Promise 65

SUSPICIOUS CONFESSIONS 73

    Chapter 1 74

    Chapter 2 80

    Chapter 3 84

Chapter 4	94
Chapter 5	97
Chapter 6	102
Chapter 7	115
Chapter 9	129

HOME FIRES BURNING 133

Chapter 1 - Fire in the Sky	134
Chapter 2 - Fire Starter	140
Chapter 3 - The Agreement	147
Chapter 4 - Suspicious Eyes	153
Chapter 5 - Another Dead End	159
Chapter 6 - September Sunday	164
Chapter 7 - Beware the Fires of Hell	171
Chapter 8 - Dangerous Discovery	176
Chapter 9 - Home Fires Burning	185

THE PLEA BARGAIN 190

Chapter 1	191
Chapter 2	199
Chapter 3	208
Chapter 4	217

Chapter 5	221
Chapter 6	234
Chapter 7	239
Chapter 8	242
Chapter 9	247

LOVES PLAIN TRUTHS ... 252

Chapter 1 - Only Child	253
Chapter 2 - Curioser and Curioser	260
Chapter 3 - Mum's the Word	266
Chapter 4 - Someone's Watching	270
Chapter 5 - A Taste of English	276
Chapter 6 - Fearful Journey	282
Chapter 7 - The Talk	289
Chapter 8 - Shots in the Dark	296
Chapter 9 - Attacked!	301
Chapter 10 - Epilogue	309

THE MYSTERIOUS DISAPEARANCE ... 318

Chapter 1	319
Chapter 2	325
Chapter 3	330

Chapter 4	337
Chapter 5	342
Chapter 6	347
Chapter 7	351
Chapter 8	358
Chapter 9	371
BONUS - Drug Of Choice	375

A NOTE FOR OUR READERS…

If you enjoy this book, make sure to sign here for information about next releases, discount offers and FREE books from Rachel H. Kester and other great clean stories authors.

Join us here completely free, and never miss all the best in the incredible world of the western romance:

http://www.cleanstories.com/rachelkester/

We look forward to reading with you ;-)

Sincerely Yours.

Amish Investigation

THE PLAIN ART OF MURDER

CHAPTER 1 - A GUT DAY GONE BAD

The dawn of the second morning of the Amish Acres Arts and Crafts festival was truly a gift from *Gott*. Rachel Miller drew deeply of the sweet air noticeably lacking the humidity so common for August in Nappanee, Indiana. It was bound to be another long busy day and Rachel was grateful it promised to be sunny and comfortable.

Rachel laid a hand on her protruding belly. Now that she was growing near the time her *bobli* would be born, the heat and humidity drained her. Today, however, was going to be a *gut* day, she could feel it.

She took another look around their vendor space, making sure everything was in place. Tables and shelves were lined with sparkling jars of pickles and relish, apple sauce, salsa, and a variety of fruit butters. Bags of golden noodles, bottles of amber honey, along with multiple cakes, cookies, and pies, were ready to sell. Many of her handwoven baskets were available and so were some beautiful needlepoint pieces.

On her husband Aaron's side of the booth gleaming handmade furnishings were displayed. Cradles and rockers shared space with a dining room set, hutch, bookcases, and a bed. Pride welled within her at the sight. It was a sim to be prideful but it was hard not to react that way when she looked at the results of her husband's skillful craftsmanship. *Gott* had truly blessed him with a special talent for woodworking.

"Rachel, *gut* morning." Rachel recognized the voice of her best friend Naomi Burkholder and turned to greet her with a warm smile.

"Gut morning and isn't it a beautiful one?"

"*Jah*, is *wunderbaar*."

Rachel tipped her head and eyed Naomi curiously. She was a pretty girl with chocolate brown curls swept up under her white *kapp*. Her complexion was smooth as cream, but there was an added tint of pink staining her cheeks today and a twinkle dancing in her eyes.

"You certainly look happy. Has something exciting happened? Perhaps you and Sam have made some decisions."

The blush on Naomi's cheeks grew even brighter. "Why would you say that?"

"Maybe because you have a special glow about you."

"Don't be silly. I'm just enjoying the festival. I've even heard rumors that my quilt is up for a big prize. Maybe even best in show."

"That is *gut* news. You deserve to win. You create the most beautiful quilts I have ever seen."

"*Danka*, Rachel. They're selling well, too, so I better hurry on to my booth and get ready to open up."

Naomi waved goodbye and Rachel went back to the business at hand. She, too, had tasks to complete before the crowds began arriving. Normally this far along in her pregnancy she wouldn't spend so much time in public, staying close to home instead. The Amish Acres Arts and Crafts Festival was one of the biggest in the country, however, and contributed significantly to their family's income so every helping hand was needed.

A few minutes later she was joined by her mother and two younger sisters. Aaron's father came striding up along with his *bruder* Eli. Everyone was ready for a busy day.

Just before the gates were s to open to the public Rachel decided she needed to pay a visit to the restroom. Her *bobli* was feeling frisky today. The little one seemed to be playing trampoline on Rachel's bladder. She needed to leave now if she was going to make it to the bathroom in time. *Ach*, it was a inconvenient part of the pregnancy process but she knew any discomfort she experienced now would be well worth the gift she would receive in the near future.

She hurried along the gravel path, nodding greetings here and there to people she knew. The only people on the grounds this early were vendors and Amish Acres personnel. There was Mrs. Yoder, a widow with eight children. Mr. Zook strode by trailed by his string of sons.

Rachel had almost neared her destination when she ran into Mary K Bontrager, a girl just a year or two younger than herself. She hoped to sidestep and keep going but Mary K stepped in front of her.

"Hello, Rachel. You're looking well." The girl's smile didn't reach her eyes as she ran her gaze over Rachel's obvious condition.

Honestly, she couldn't remember a time when Mary ever really looked happy. She always seemed nervous and perturbed. She was a big girl, tall with a strong body, but the usual frown she wore diminished her looks. Normally she spoke little but today she seemed inclined to chat.

"How is your family?"

"They're *gut*, Mary K. And yours?

"*Gut*, also. So are you enjoying the festival?"

"*Jah*, very much. It's hard work but it's always interesting. It was *gut* to see you, but now I must go."

"Where are you off to in such a hurry? I thought you might join me for a *kaffe*." She spoke the words to Rachel but glanced nervously over her shoulder at the same time.

"I would love to, Mary, but I must get to the restroom and then back to our booth. I do not want to be away too long and leave all the work to *Maemm* and the girls. You understand, I'm sure." Mary K nodded but made no move to step out of Rachel's way. Finally she moved around the girl and continued up the path.

This restroom was small with only two stalls. The door to the handicap stall was closed but the other one was vacant and Rachel hurried in to it. She was seated on the stool when she glanced down at her swollen ankles. That's when she saw it. A white Amish *kapp* crumpled on the floor of the next stall.

And next to it a pool of long brown curls spilled across the tiles.

CHAPTER 2 - CRIME SCENE

Rachel froze, her breath trapped in throat.

"Hello. Are you okay?" Her voice echoed in the tiny building. "Are you all right?"

No answer.

Rachel dragged her clothes back into place and pushed out of her stall and banged on the other door.

"You in there. Do you need help?"

The only answer was silence.

The door was locked but Rachel had to know who was in there. Awkwardly she lowered herself to her knees, one hand supporting her pregnant belly. She bent over as best she could and peered under the stall door.

Naomi. *Gott* help her it was Naomi Burkholder.

Rachel reached under the door and grabbed her friends arm, shaking it and calling her name over and over. There was no response and the arm fell limply to the floor when she let it go.

She was just hurt, Rachel assured herself. Everything would be fine. Naomi just needed help. She'd be all right. She couldn't be…dead.

Getting back to her feet was even harder than getting down. She had to crawl to a sink to help her stand. For a moment the world whirled around her but Rachel swallowed three times and drew in a deep breath. She had to get help. Get help for Naomi. The thought pounded in her head like a drum.

Then she was running. She threw the door open and raised her skirts, sprinting towards the nearest vendor.

"Help. I need help. I found my friend in the bathroom. She's hurt." She tried to keep her voice calm so the man she spoke to could understand her. "Please."

When her words sank into his conscience the baldheaded man's eyes bulged and he waved his wife over.

"Dori, go with this woman. I'll call security. Hurry now."

Rachel and the older woman ran back to the restroom. Dori was tiny and managed to crawl under the door of the stall where Naomi lay. After just a moment she unlocked the door, her face ashen.

"Honey, she's dead." The woman's hands gripped Rachel's upper arms tightly but Rachel didn't even feel it. Numbness settled over her. She couldn't hear anything the sound of dozens of bees swarming through her head and for a moment the world threatened to go black.

A crowd of people surged into the tiny space all at once and Rachel had to get out of there. In a frantic race to exit she pushed against the people trying to enter. The contents of her stomach churned violently. Not Naomi, *Gott*, not dear, gentle Naomi.

At last she managed to escape to the fresh air and grabbed hold of a stout tree for support. A hundred questions swirled through her mind. What could have happened? Did she have a stroke, an aneurysm? Why would a seemingly perfectly healthy young woman like Naomi just drop dead in a restroom? There were too many questions and no answers. She slammed her fist to her lips and bit down on her fingers, hard. Otherwise she might scream.

Word spread quickly through the festival grounds. A golf cart arrived carrying Naomi's parents, their faces stern and unreadable, Mrs. Burkholder's face devoid of color.

Moments later Rachel's own family came hustling up, surrounding her in their midst. Aaron moved close to her side, a worried expression painting his features. *Maemm* and *Daett* both murmured words of comfort, *Maemm* reaching for her cold hands. Rachel still couldn't comprehend all they were saying but she felt better, stronger, with her loved ones close by.

Police arrived in force, pushing the crowds back, quickly taping off a large area. An organized frenzy followed, detectives scurrying around like busy ants. Rachel noted her friend Detective Abby Hale seemed to be in charge. She met Abby in a class on canning and preserving that she was helping teach and the two women, despite their different backgrounds, quickly became friends.

It wasn't long before Abby approached her family gathered underneath the shady maple tree. Dressed in black slacks and a short-sleeved white blouse, topped by a gray jacket. Abby dressed every bit the professional, but that didn't change the fact that she looked more like a nymph than a police officer. A cap of feathery red hair framed a gamin face. Her body was petite. She probably didn't weigh more than 98 pounds and normally her emerald green eyes were alight with mischief. Not today, though. Now her face wore a blended expression of sympathy and gravity.

"Rachel, I'm so sorry about your friend."

"*Danka*, Abby. I still can't believe she's gone."

"I know it's got to be a shock. You and Naomi were close, weren't you?"

"*Jah*. We have been best friends since we were toddling." Rachel's voice choked and she fought to control it. "I loved her like another sister."

"I am so, so, sorry, Rach. And I hate to add to your woes, but I need to talk to you privately. I mean, you found her, you were close to her. I need answers to some questions."

The news caused a slight tremor to ripple through Rachel's body. She wasn't ready to talk about it. She wanted to plead for more time, for Abby to let her rest for a few hours and collect her senses. Her mind was still whirling like a windmill in a tornado.

"As soon as possible." Maybe Abby could read her thoughts? She had kyboshed the idea of waiting until later before Rachel even voiced it.

"Can Aaron come with me?" She sounded fragile even to her own ears.

"Aaron, but no one else," Abby agreed, worrying that the shock Rachel had endured could cause problems with her pregnancy. She was confident Aaron Miller was an honest man who didn't gossip and Rachel needed him with her now. "Let's go sit in my car where we can turn the air conditioning on and be comfortable. I'll pick up some sodas for us on the way."

CHAPTER 3 - ACCUSED

There really was no choice. Rachel reluctantly followed behind Abby, Aaron close by her side. Although they never indulged in public displays of affection because it violated the *Ordnung* just his nearness comforted Rachel. She drew on his strength, confident in his love.

Abby handed them each a tall paper cup of icy cold cola she'd purchased at a vendor then led them to an inconspicuous gray sedan. Rachel sank into the passenger seat with a groan, luxuriating in the rare feel of cool blowing air. Her body ached, rife with tension, her swollen feet and ankles grateful for the rest.

"I'm going to record our conversation just so I don't forget anything, okay, Rachel?" Abby sat a small recording device on the dashboard of the car and Rachel nodded silently.

"So tell me, did anything feel off when you approached the restroom? Did you see anyone hanging around or looking out of place?"

Rachel thought carefully about the question then shook her head.

"When was the last time you saw Naomi before you found her in the restroom?"

"I spoke to her just this morning. She was passing by our booth space and stopped to say hello."

"Did everything appear normal about her? Did she seemed worried or upset about anything? Was she feeling okay?"

"She was fine. She seemed happy, almost joyful." The vision of Naomi's smiling face floated before Rachel's eyes. "In fact, I would say she was even more cheerful than usual."

Abby's finely arched brows dipped in a frown as she thought about Rachel's answers to her questions. She nibbled at her lower lip, a sure sign she was concentrating.

"Abby, what is it? Do you know what happened to Naomi?" Urgency tinted Rachel's question. She needed answers. Now.

Abby drew in a deep breath before she spoke, leveling a serious gaze at both Aaron and Rachel.

"What I'm about to tell you can go no further than this car for now. We'll make a public statement later. Can I count on you both to keep this confidential?"

"Of course." Aaron answered first.

"Absolutely." Rachel echoed his vow in a solemn tone.

"Naomi did not die from natural causes. She was murdered. Strangled."

Abby's words fell like raining bricks thundering down in Rachel's mind.

Murdered.

Why? Who would want poor sweet Rachel dead? The questions reverberated through Rachel's head, pounding out a demand for answers. What kind of devil did this to a sweet, innocent girl. What kind of evil dwelt within a murderer's soul?

"Rachel, I have to ask you. Did you and Naomi have any problems? Any disagreements or harsh words between you lately?"

Rachel shook her head vigorously.

"No, not at all. We were friends. Best friends. We never argued."

"I had to ask you. You may have been the last person to see Naomi alive beside her killer."

Aaron sat up straighter in the back seat.

"What are you trying to say, detective?"

Abby didn't flinch when he questioned her.

"What I'm saying is the last person to see the victim alive is often the first person suspected of the crime."

RACHEL SAT on the side of the bed and hugged herself. Despite the warmth of the August evening and the soft weight of her flannel nightgown she was cold; freezing cold. Shivers racked her body and goosebumps covered her arms.

Naomi was dead. Murdered. The idea was barely fathomable. Even more ludicrous was the hint that Rachel could be a suspect in the murder. When Abby made that statement Aaron openly guffawed.

"Does she look in any condition to kill someone? To strangle them to death?" Rachel could hear the anger in his voice, thickly tinted with disbelief.

"I'm not saying she killed Naomi, Aaron. I'm just saying she'll need to make a formal statement and tell us everything she knows."

"But that's just it, Abby. I don't know anything. I wish I did. Believe me, I want to know who did this to her. Right now that is my dearest wish."

And it truly was. There was a burning desire deep in Rachel's soul to know the identity of this heartless killer. To discover who had thrown away Rachel's future, her entire life. And why. She knew she would never truly rest until she had the answers to her questions.

Aaron strode into the room and sat down next to her, his arm wrapping around her shoulders drawing her close to him. Rachel cuddled gratefully against his warmth. Aaron's hand moved to rest on her belly just as the *bobli* delivered a healthy kick. A look of delight lit up his handsome face, his brown eyes softening with wonder.

"That is the kick of a fine strong son, I think." Aaron rubbed his palm across her firm flesh.

"Or it might be a healthy daughter poking you." Her finger drilled into his ribs, making him jerk as she tickled him.

"A fine healthy girl that would grow up to be a good woman, a loving woman." A shudder of emotion rippled through Rachel. "A fine young woman like Rachel."

The tears broke free then, escaping from her in great bursting sobs, the force shuddering through her entire body.

"Why, Aaron? I just don't understand why?"

Aaron quickly drew her to him, holding her firmly in his arms.

"Hush, now, *fraa*. Don't cry." Aaron ran a calloused hand down her back, caressing the waterfall of auburn waves that fell to her waistline. "Now is the time you must rely on *Gott*, trust in Him to reveal the answers in His time."

"I will, husband. But maybe, don't you think, this is one time when *Gott* might appreciate a little help from us?"

"He will reveal everything we need to know in His time, Rachel." Aaron repeated. "Let *Gott* do His job and the police do theirs."

A flame of rebellion flickered to life deep in Rachel's belly. She would trust in *Gott*, she would rely on the trained professionals to deal with this case, but that didn't mean she was obligated to sit back and do nothing. She wanted this murderer exposed. The sin should be revealed so others could beware the hands of a killer.

"But I feel driven to find the answers, to find out why Naomi had to die." Her voice shook with her conviction.

"Rachel, my *fraa,* you have a bigger cause right now. Now you must focus on bringing our *bobli* into the world. *Gott* has blessed us with the priceless gift of a child and you need to concentrate on your health and our child's health. Others will find the answers you seek."

But Rachel didn't want to wait for others. She wanted answers now and silently vowed to do everything she could to find Naomi's killer. After all, *Gott* helps those who help themselves.

CHAPTER 4 - TOO MANY QUESTIONS, NOT ENOUGH ANSWERS

Rachel slept little that night. Between the baby tossing and turning restlessly and the haunting dreams that taunted her, she felt more tired when she arose then when she went to bed. Her legs felt like lead as she dragged herself to the kitchen to start the *kaffe*.

Much to her surprise Aaron was there before her, pouring a cup of the fragrant brew. He held it out to her and she accepted it gratefully. *Gott* truly had blessed her with an exceptional husband. She shot a prayer of thanksgiving towards the skies for her many gifts.

"Do you feel up to going to the festival today?" Aaron asked as he moved to sit at the table. "You certainly don't have to if you'd rather not."

Rachel considered the question for a long moment. On one hand, she would love to stay at home and hide from reality. Her back hurt, her feet were swollen, and there was a tension pulling behind her eyes. And she needed to call on the Burkholder family as well. She'd take them a basketful of cookies and muffins and express her heartfelt sympathies.

But another part of her urged her to go to the festival. It would give her a chance to question people, to poke and prod into Naomi's murder. She had every confidence in Abby's ability as a detective, but the Amish were a close knit community. She felt confident people of her order would speak more freely to her than they would a police officer.

"I think I should go to the festival," she finally replied. "I'd rather not be alone today."

Her decision made Rachel hurried to dress in a plain navy blue dress with a lighter blue apron topping it. She wasted little time plaiting her auburn hair into a braid, coiling it into a bun, and covering it with her *kapp*. After a hurried breakfast of canned peaches and oatmeal she and Aaron headed to the buggy that Aaron had hitched up while she cooked. Soon they were trotting towards Amish Acres, sunshine lighting the country road.

"I want you to take it easy today." Aaron couldn't hide the concern he felt for her. This was their first child and the whole concept of labor and delivery was scary enough. He didn't need the additional worry of Rachel playing detective. "Your time is near. You need to be careful."

"Yes, Aaron," she replied obediently. After all, it wouldn't be too stressful to talk to a few people, ask a few questions. She had thought about this for hours and had a few suspects in mind.

The killer could be Sam Shultz, the young blacksmith who was courting Naomi. Rachel knew he'd had some issues with Naomi enjoying her *rumpsringe*, her running around time. Naomi had confided in her that he'd shown signs of jealousy because she had been spending time with Mike Calloway, the owner of an art gallery where Naomi displayed her quilted pieces.

Or maybe that theory could work in reverse. Perhaps Calloway was resentful because Naomi refused to commit to a relationship with him? That decision would mean she would have to leave her church, be shunned by her family and friends. Rachel couldn't see Naomi willingly giving up those lifelong ties.

Rachel hurried through the work of restocking the shelves in the space, her mind continuing to play across provoking questions like a tongue continues to scrape across a sharp edge on a tooth. She had trouble focusing on her tasks and *Maemm* had to call her name twice to get her attention. Finally Esther stopped what she was doing and rested her hand on her daughter's back.

"Rachel, my *dochtah*, I know you are troubled."

Tears burned behind her lids, her eyes cast downward as she nodded. "I just don't understand, *Maemm*, I don't understand why Naomi is dead. I guess part of it is selfishness because even though I know she is with our *Gott* my heart aches because I will miss her so."

"That is a natural part of mourning. We celebrate our loved one's passage to the Promised Land but we grieve our own earthly loss." *Maemm's* gentle face was solemn, her hand warm on Rachel's shoulder.

"Yes, but that's only part of it. I mean, if Naomi had died a natural death it would hurt, but it would be easier to understand. But you know it was announced last night that Naomi was murdered. Someone killed her." Rachel was careful not to reveal the cause of death. That information was still under wraps. "I keep wondering who, why. And I keep picturing poor Naomi. Did she suffer? Did she see it coming? Did she fight for her life and know she was going to die? She must have been so terrified."

"Do not let your mind focus on those negative thoughts, *dochtah*. No *gut* will come from it." The older woman took Rachel's hands in her own, squeezing them gently. "There are times in life when we must just put it in *Gott's* hands. When I am feeling troubled I like to remember one of my favorite verses from Psalm 16: *I keep my eyes on the Lord. With him at my right hand I will not be shaken.*"

Rachel drew in a deep shuddering breath. She would keep her eyes on the Lord. She would trust Him to hold her steady and see her through this.

But she still wanted to find the answers now. If stubbornness was a sin, Rachel knew she was guilty.

CHAPTER 5 - CLUELESS

The murder of a young Amish woman didn't seem to diminish the crowd at the festival. Tourists thronged the area, buying up merchandise and taking pictures. Many of the Englishers were friendly, some of them asking questions about the Amish way of life. There were always a few, though, that rudely pointed at the Plain people, making fun of their dress and their language.

Rachel was used to it and normally it didn't bother her but today a teenage boy with blue hair pointed at her belly and said, "Would you look at that? She's prego. I didn't think Amish chicks did the horizontal boogie."

He and his friends hooted and hollered like he'd made a great joke. Rachel felt fire flaming in her cheeks, unmitigated anger surging through her veins. She wanted to fly at them, scream at them, make them ashamed of their crude behavior, but that was wrong. It would bring shame to her and shame to her family to show such loss of control.

Then Aaron was at her side, towering protectively over her. The heated glare he shot at the boys could have melted nails and they hastily beat a retreat.

"Well, there are some advantages to being giant-sized," he chuckled, offering her his special grin, the one he saved only for her; then he grew more serious. "You are tired, Rachel. Would you like to go home?"

She shook her head. "No, but I could use a break. I think I'll walk around for a bit."

Aaron lifted his straw hat and wiped the sweat off his forehead. "Don't overdo it. It's hot today."

"I won't be gone long. I promise."

Rachel really did need a break and a walk gave her an excuse to stroll amongst the other exhibits. She remembered what Naomi said about being in the running for Best of Show. Could one of her competitors have killed her? Rachel hated to think her friend might have been killed over only $1000, but people had murdered for less.

She rambled through the exhibits of other quilt artists, Amish and English alike. She stopped to speak with Rebekah Gruber, another friend of her and Naomi's.

"Isn't it sad about Naomi?" Rebekah was the first to bring up the subject.

Rachel nodded, picking up a colorful quilted pillow on display. The workmanship was remarkable, almost as good as Naomi's.

"I can't believe she was murdered. Who would do such a thing?" Rebekah's voice trembled a bit as she spoke.

"I would like to know the answer to that question, too." Rachel turned the pillow over and examined the other side. "Her stall is right next to yours. Did you see anyone in particular talking to her the day before yesterday or yesterday morning? Anyone acting angry or odd?"

"No, I don't think so…" Rebekah tilted her head, her hazel eyes thoughtful. "Oh, of course there were the usual festival goers. And Sam stopped by. They talked for a couple minutes, it looked like they might have been discussing something important. But he didn't seem angry."

"Think hard, Rebekah. Anyone else?"

"Well there were lots of people passing by, many from the community stopped to say hello. I remember seeing Mrs. Sawyer, the Methodist preacher's wife, and nurse Ruby Anderson, Mike Calloway, the art gallery owner, and that man who has the camera shop. Lots of people, Rachel, but nobody seemed upset about anything. And Naomi was in good spirits all day."

"What about competitors in her class? Anyone showing an unusual interest in her work?"

"No one I know of. I was busy, you know? I wasn't spending all my time watching Naomi."

Rachel sighed with frustration. She was getting nowhere. The answers to her questions were still as elusive as bubbles floating through the air. She headed back to her own booth, her hand holding her back to ease the growing pain there. Maybe Aaron was right. Maybe she should go home. She could take the buggy and Aaron could catch a ride home with *Daett*. Her parents just lived next door to Rachel's own home.

Her family watched her with concern as she made her excuses. Aaron walked with her to where their buggy waited and patted his horse Sampson's shoulder.

"You take extra care going home, boy. You're transporting mighty special cargo." He turned and winked at Rachel before offering her a hand into the carriage. "And you should take a nap when you get there. I know you did not sleep well last night"

His voice was gruff but the look in his eyes was tender. Once again Rachel felt a swell of gratitude within her. She was so blessed to have such a kind and caring husband.

Rachel nodded her head and clucked to Sampson to head out. She drove carefully, seeming to be the only vehicle leaving instead of coming. When she finally reached the exit, though, she had a sudden whim. Instead of turning towards home she headed into town.

After a short drive she pulled the buggy up to a hitching post on the main street. Right in front of Calloway's Country Art Gallery. Mike Calloway was on her list of suspects and she wanted to talk to him. Of course, she couldn't come right out and ask him if he'd killed Naomi, but she could possibly glean some bit of information. She'd just have to use the brain *Gut* had given her.

CHAPTER 6 - ANOTHER DEAD END

A bell tinkled over the door when Rachel pushed through it. She stepped into a cool, spacious room filled with photographs and paintings, painted saw blades, metalwork, needlepoint, and a selection of Amish made quilts. She headed directly towards the colorful coverlets.

"Good afternoon. Mrs. Miller isn't it?" A tall, slender man greeted her as he came into the room from someplace in the back of the building. Mike Calloway was probably considered handsome by most women, but Rachel though him a little too charming, a hint of arrogance surrounding him. The spicy-sweet smell of his cologne wafted to Rachel's nose and she sneezed. Twice.

"Excuse me." She tried not to breath in deeply; the scent was almost cloying.

"You're a friend of Naomi's aren't you?" At her nod he continued. "I cannot tell you how sorry I am for your loss. Such a shame. A lovely young woman and so talented."

"Yes, I am saddened by her passing. That is one of the reasons I am here today. I wondered if you have any of Naomi's quilts left. Have they all been sold?"

He smiled sadly. "Her pieces always went quickly. I do have one, however. Would you like to see it?"

"Yes, please."

Rachel noticed that he almost seemed to glide, rather than walk across the hardwood floor. His crepe soled shoes made little noise. It would certainly be easy enough for him to sneak up on an unsuspecting person.

"Here it is." Mike stopped before a wooden quilt rack and gently unfolded the coverlet. The pattern was of falling autumn leaves, richly hued with ambers, golds, and cranberries, an exquisite example of Naomi's skill. Rachel reached out and stroked the soft fabric. How hard Naomi must have worked on this piece, her delicate stitches nearly invisible. She also noted the $1500 price tag discreetly tucked in the corner.

"You sold several of Naomi's pieces, didn't you?"

"Sure did. Anything she brought me flew out the door. I've only got this piece left because she just delivered it a day or two before..." He didn't finish the statement but

Rachel knew he meant just a day or two before she was murdered.

"She told me you and she had become friends. That you talked about many things."

"That is true. I enjoyed listening to her tell me about things that inspired her creativity with her needle. And I think she liked hearing a bit about the outside world."

"Tell me, did you get the chance to visit the festival yet?"

"Yes, I made a point of it. It's a great place to find new talent for the gallery." He leaned against a wooden counter and crossed his arms across his sky blue polo shirt. "In fact, I was there shortly after Naomi's body was found."

His words smacked Rachel like a club. So he may have been on the grounds when Naomi was killed.

"Did you know that I am the one who found her body?" Rachel tilted her head up and looked him directly in the eye. He met her gaze for a moment then looked away.

"No, I hadn't heard that. It must have been awful for you."

"I'd say that's putting it mildly. She was my best friend and always had been."

"Again, my condolences." He crushed the quilt he held to him for a moment then extended it towards Rachel. "Here. For you."

Stunned, Rachel made no move to take it. "I cannot accept such an expensive gift."

"Please." For a moment his eyes clouded with grief. "I know how fond she was of you. She talked to me about your friendship. She would want you to have this."

A FEW MINUTES later she walked out of the store with the tissue-wrapped quilt tucked securely inside a Calloway's shopping bag. Now she was even more confused. Was the quilt a gift of condolence…or a gift to ease a guilty conscience?

She had just reached her buggy when she heard a voice call her name. Turning, she saw Abby hurrying up the street towards her.

"Rachel, hi. How are you holding up?"

Rachel managed a smile for her friend. "Well, I'm feeling fat, I can guarantee you that."

"Who are you kidding, girlfriend? You're absolutely beautiful. But you do look hot. Come on, let's have some ice tea before you hit the road."

"Sounds good. I meant to come by your office before I went home, anyway."

The two women headed into a café next door to the gallery and selected an isolated booth away from other customers.

"I'm guessing you were coming see me to find out if I know any more about Naomi's death." Abby waited to bring up the subject until the waitress brought their drinks and left their table. They each took long pulls on their straws before continuing their conversation.

"Right on the first try, Detective. Not knowing who did this to her is eating at me like a rat gnawing at a chicken carcass."

"We're doing everything possible, Rachel. The autopsy confirmed she was strangled, like I said, but revealed little else. I've interviewed dozens of people, including all her family members."

"Did you talk to Sam Shultz? Or Mike Calloway?"

Abby ran her hand across her chin in frustration. "Yes and yes. I even talked to the vendor who served her coffee yesterday morning. No one seems to have any clue who would want to hurt Naomi *and* they all have alibis for the time of her death."

"I've been asking some questions of my own but I haven't learned any more than you have.

Abby eyed her sternly. "You need to stay out of this, young lady. Killers are nobody to tangle with, especially not in your condition."

Rachel opened her mouth to voice a protest but just then Abby's cell phone rang. The detective pulled it from her pocket and answered the call. For a moment she didn't say anything, just listened, her face hardening by the moment.

All she said was "I'll be right there," before she disconnected the call and slid out of the booth.

"Go home, Rachel. Go home and stay there."

"Why, Abby? What's wrong?" Rachel awkwardly maneuvered her rounded belly under the tabletop and rose to her feet.

Abby didn't say anything for a long moment then heaved a deep sigh.

"They've found another body. Another dead Amish girl. Sarah Kaufman."

CHAPTER 7 - AND THEN THERE WERE TWO

Rachel had to pull the buggy off the road twice and vomit violently before she reached home. She'd just stepped into the kitchen after getting the buggy unhitched and Sampson in his stall before Aaron arrived, his features twisted with worry.

"Rachel." He slammed through the screen door and skidded to a stop in front of her. She knew at once by the look on his face that he'd heard the news.

"It's happened again. Another girl killed. This time sweet Sarah Kaufman." Rachel's hands covered her mouth in horror. "She's Naomi's cousin."

"*Jah*, how did you know?"

"I stopped in town for a few minutes before I came home," she confessed. "I was with Abby when she got the call."

"Rachel." He stepped closer and grasped both her shoulders in his hands. "This could be a serial killer. You will not go anywhere alone as long as this madman is on the loose. Understand?" He looked her straight in her eyes, awaiting her answer.

"But, Aaron…"

"No buts. I won't have you out there alone, defenseless against a crazy man. You owe it to our child to keep him safe."

"Or her."

"Or her. But you must obey me on this. Do not leave this house alone. Someone will go with you anywhere you need to go. Understand?"

AARON INSISTED she lay down and nap but sleep wouldn't come. After an hour of trying to rest she got up and went to the kitchen to start supper. Through the open window she could hear the sound of Aaron's axe as he chopped wood, the steady thumping a sure sign he was troubled. Aaron often split logs when he was disturbed about something. Rachel understood how he felt. She, too, needed to be busy.

She would feed him well tonight. She managed a small smile as she remembered *Maemm* saying a man always felt better with a full stomach. Aaron loved her fried chicken and mashed potatoes and gravy so that is what she would make even if it would heat up the house somewhat. There were also green beans, fresh tomatoes and cucumbers from the garden, and she'd open one of the jars of spiced apples she put up last fall.

"I wonder if the killer has something against that particular family." She asked the question out loud as she turned the sizzling chicken in the cast iron skillet. She mulled the question over. That was one possibility. Or could it be that the killer just had a penchant for slender, dark haired Amish girls? Naomi and Sarah's mothers were sisters and the two cousins shared a strong family resemblance. Both tall and willowy, each with shiny dark brown curls and the same dancing dimples. Even their voices sounded alike.

Had sounded alike she reminded herself, shaking her head. Thinking of Naomi and Sarah in the past tense sent a pain zinging through her heart. Well, she better get used to it. Nothing could change the fact that they were gone.

AARON PUSHED his chair back from the table and groaned, one hand rubbing his belly.

"That was a fine meal, Mrs. Miller You have got one lucky husband."

"Don't I know it," Rachel teased as she stood to begin clearing the table. Before she could pick up the first plate, though, she found herself being pulled down into Aaron's lap. Her arms wrapped around his neck and she rested her head on his shoulder. They sat like that for a long moment, not speaking, just reveling in their closeness, their aliveness.

"I can't imagine the pain Naomi and Sarah's families must be suffering." Aaron murmured into her ear. "The very thought of losing you or the little one you carry is unimaginable."

Before Rachel could answer a bang on the front door was followed by a female voice.

"Anyone home?"

"It's Abby." Rachel hauled her body off Aaron's lap, a blush tinting her cheeks. She ran her hands down her apron to rid herself of imaginary wrinkles then hurried towards the door.

"Abby, please, come in. Would you like some tea?"

Abby stepped into the room, her small shoulders slumped. "That sounds heavenly about now, Rachel. Thank you."

"Here, have a seat." Aaron followed Rachel into the front room as she carried in the tea and waved Abby towards his favorite rocker. "Have you news for us?"

"I'm afraid we don't know much. Sarah left early this morning to make her regular weekly egg delivery and then she was going on to the festival. When the horse and buggy returned home without her, her family became worried and sent her brother John to look for her. He found her in a ditch about a mile from their house."

Rachel's hand crept to her throat. "Was she…"

"Strangled. Just like Naomi."

"So she was murdered, too. It was no accident." Aaron made it a statement, not a question.

"Yes." Abby ran her hand through her cap of coppery curls. "And it looks like the work of the same killer."

Rachel sank into a straight-backed chair, her heart sinking even lower.

"Does that mean there is a serial killer at large?" Rachel's voice was barely above a whisper but she looked directly into Abby's eyes. She would not flinch from the truth.

The two women locked gazes for several long minutes before Abby replied.

"We're not going to jump to any conclusions. We're investigating every possible angle. There is the family angle to look at as well since both victims were related…But yes, one theory is this could be the work of a serial killer."

CHAPTER 8 - DARK DAYS

Amish are usually buried three days after their death but because the cousins died so close together it was decided there would only be one funeral for both girls to take place on the third day after Naomi's demise. Since Naomi's home was bigger the visitation and funeral would be held there.

Rachel wanted to help with the funeral preparations. Her mother and sisters felt the same way so *Daett* and Rachel's three brothers escorted the women to the Burkholder's and the Kaufmann's. Aaron had been asked to build the coffins so he remained in his workshop preparing the simple pine boxes used for Amish funerals.

The weather had returned to hot and humid and a layer of gray clouds seemed to hover in place in the windless sky. Rachel was sweating before she even left the house that morning.

When the buggy pulled up in front Rachel was ready. She'd filled two baskets with loaves of fresh baked zucchini bread, jars of peach butter, and containers of chicken and noodles. She added an apple pie to each basket and covered them with red and whited checked cloths.

Esther had also brought plenty of food for the bereaved families.

"Your sisters made the cookies," *Maemm* told Rachel. "They're turning into excellent bakers."

Fourteen-year-old Emma and 15-year old Miriam both blushed at their mother's praise. They were pretty girls dark hair and dark eyes. The thought bothered Rachel more than she liked to admit. Naomi and Sarah were both tall and slender, both brunettes - and some crazy person had chosen girls who looked them as his murder victims. An icy fist of fear clenched Rachel's heart. This killer must be caught. If not, one of her sisters could become his next target.

Naomi had been one of eight children, falling near the middle of the pack. The Burkholder house was crowded with sisters and brothers and their children, grandparents, and aunts and uncles. Rachel spotted Naomi's parents and went first to speak with them.

As was customary for the Amish the older Burkholder's kept their emotions under control, but Rachel saw the pain in Naomi's *Maemm's* eyes, the sallowness of her *Daett's* complexion. There were some signs of grief that couldn't be hidden no matter how hard one tried.

The tone was subdued as Rachel and her family pitched in to help prepare the house for the visitation and the funeral service. The men went about removing the furniture from the room where the caskets would be placed as was customary for their people. While they did that the women gathered in the kitchen preparing food that would be served at the traditional after funeral dinner. Hams were baked and potato salads, coleslaw, and macaroni salads were prepared and stored in propane operated refrigerators.

The kitchen was a busy place but the women worked together like a well-organized team. They had all been here and done this before. Death was a natural part of life so funerals were not rare. This double ceremony was unique, though. These girls were victims of some insane person, a sick, perverted mind. That thought seemed to be weighing heavily on everyone and it was a much more subdued atmosphere than you would normally find in a room full of Amish women.

Rachel pushed the last of the carrot sticks she had just finished peeling into a jar of cold water and closed the lid. After placing it in the refrigerator she rubbed the palms of her hands across the small of her back. The ache there was now almost a constant companion and the heat in the kitchen added to her discomfort. Maybe she would step outside for a few minutes and try to find a breeze to cool her off.

As soon as she walked out the screen door she realized her quest was hopeless. The humidity added a thickness to the air that made it hard to breathe, the heat slapping her in her face. Still optimistic she walked further from the house towards the shade of a towering oak tree.

The widespread limbs provided a bit of relief from the sun and Rachel leaned tiredly against the broad tree trunk. Fatigue sank into every cell of her body. She was hot, tired, and depressed.

And she was scared.

Frightened of what might happen next. Fearful that someone else would die before the killer could be stopped.

Be strong and courageous. Do not be afraid or terrified because of them, for the Lord your Gott goes with you, he will never leave you nor forsake you. The verse from Deuteronomy 31:6 popped into Rachel's mind and she grasped onto it like a lifeline. She would not fear. *Gott's* will would be done. And she had no doubt that killer would be unmasked, his sins revealed.

Jah, a tiny voice in her head seemed to mock her, challenging her faith, *but will it be in time to prevent the death of another innocent young girl?*

Rachel tried to fight the doubts plaguing her mind; she couldn't let them fester. Doubts were poisonous to the soul. Faith should be unwavering, unshakeable. Rachel must draw deep within her to fling away those fears and trust in the Lord.

The sound of an approaching buggy broke into her thoughts and Rachel turned to see who was coming. She recognized Sam Shultz at the reins of a chestnut mare.

Rachel stayed hidden behind the tree for a moment, watching Naomi's suitor climb down from the buggy seat and hitch the horse to a post. She noted his face was the image of despair, brows furrowed, lips downturned. His shoulders slumped and the usual energy had gone out of his step.

He looked like the picture of a grieving suitor, weighed down by grief. She sucked in her breath as Sam paused for a moment, his hand going up to shield his face as a single sob racked through him.

Was this the portrait of a grieving man who had lost the woman he loved? Or was this a man consumed by guilt for what he had done to Naomi?

But why would he have killed Sarah?

CHAPTER 9 - A LAST GOODBYE

The morning of the funeral services dawned appropriately grey and dark to match Rachel's mood. There was nothing happy to anticipate on this day.

She dragged herself from bed, moaning as the pain in her lower back throbbed when she moved. She padded downstairs barefoot, her feet and ankles swollen to nearly twice their normal size. Dear *Gott*, she would be glad when she gave birth and began to feel more like her usual self. She was ready to hold her *bobli* in her arms.

Aaron was already up and outside taking care of chores so she needed to get breakfast started This was going to be a long day and they needed food to fortify them for the painful hours to come. Quickly she got bacon frying and began to prepare a batch of scrambled eggs. But by the time Aaron came inside and she brought a plate of hot biscuits to the table she knew she would not be able to eat a bite. If she tried she would soon be holding her head over a basin and upchucking anything she had consumed.

Aaron eyed her worriedly, a frown tugging his brows downward.

"Rachel, perhaps we should not go to the services. You are so near your time I'm sure everyone would understand our absence."

Rachel whirled on him, her face an angry mask.

"Absolutely not. I will not miss my chance to say a last goodbye to my best friend." She squared her jaw, ready to fight him about this point. She clenched her arms angrily over her protruding belly. "Don't you see, Aaron? I must go. I have to see her one more time."

Aaron eyed her solemnly before replying.

"Very well, *Fraa*, we'll go. But if you begin to feel ill or if it is too much of a strain on you, we'll come home immediately. Agreed?"

"Agreed." Rachel nodded, a little of the tension easing from her body.

By the time they left for the services Rachel had dressed in traditional Amish funeral garb. She fastened the hook and eye closure of her black dress and topped it with a black cape. A black bonnet covered the braid wound at the back of her head.

Aaron, also dressed in black, waited to help Rachel into the carriage. They spoke little as the horse trotted along the country road, each of them lost in their own thoughts.

The pasture was already filled with dozens of horses and buggies when they arrived at the Burkholder's home. Children dashed here and there across the yard and men stood in groups beneath the shady trees. A rooster crowed its cocky call in the background.

Rachel's legs trembled as she approached the caskets in the big parlor of the house. The sight of the once bright and lively Naomi laying so still, so pale, next to her equally immobile cousin, seared itself in Rachel's conscious. Both girls were dressed in white, their faces serene in death, looking like frozen angels. Rachel stood between the two caskets for a long time, thanking *Gott* for taking them home to His kingdom, yet grieving for the abrupt and violent end to their earthly lives.

The funeral service lasted two hours, filled with *Gott*'s praises and thanks for His promise of everlasting life. By the time it was over Rachel sagged with fatigue, her backache intensifying to a near unbearable force. Her feet throbbed, her sides ached, and the heat and humidity sapped every ounce of strength from her body. She was actually grateful to sink into the seat of the buggy for the ride to the simple Amish cemetery.

As they said the final goodbyes to the two women who died much too young, gray thunderclouds brooded overhead. Rachel watched the angry skies roiling and her stomach imitated the churning movements. She swallowed repeatedly to fight down the bile that kept threatening to rise in her throat.

At last it was time to head back to the house for the funeral dinner. For a while Rachel was able to turn off her tumultuous thoughts by focusing on helping to set out the food for the hoard of hungry mourners gathered together in the big barn.

Just before it was time to announce the meal was ready to be served, she remembered the jugs of lemonade she had left in the buggy. She hesitated on the back porch, eyeing the threatening skies. Any moment now they would open up and rain would come pouring down. She probably just had time to make it to the pasture where the buggies were parked before the deluge began. She headed quickly across the lawn, nearly stumbling when a loud clap of thunder made her jerk sharply.

She hadn't gotten quite as far as their buggy when the skies opened up and stinging raindrops began to hammer against her skin. It took only seconds for the downpour to drench her, beating against her like a thousand tiny hammers pounding against her flesh.

No time to go any further, she decided. She'd duck into the other barn over there where wagons were stored and wait for the worst of the storm to let up.

The wind gusted and flattened her skirt against her calves as she struggled to drag the heavy door open and she never even noticed when it knocked the bonnet from her head. Its buffeting force fought her efforts but she managed to heave old door open just wide enough to slip into the darkened space. She shivered as she escaped the cold, pounding rain and breathed a sigh of relief as she shook out her soaked skirt. The sudden storm had a ferocity that exposed Mother Nature's powerful force.

"Hello, Rachel."

Rachel nearly leapt out of her shoes when the voice came towards her from the back of the building. She turned so fast she almost lost her balance, squinting to recognize the form she saw hidden in the shadows.

"It's me, Mary K."

"Mary K, you nearly scared the life out of me." Rachel slapped one hand over her pounding heart when she recognized Mary Bontrager approaching. "I didn't know anyone else was in here."

"I just needed someplace to be alone for a minute, you know?" Mary stepped closer to her and Rachel could see she had been crying. Her damp apron was a sodden ball clutched in her fists, her black dress snug on her muscular frame. She'd taken off her *kapp* and her nut brown hair was coming loose from its pins, straggling around her broad face.

"I understand. This has been a stressful day for all of us. I think even my *bobli* is aware of the tension. It feels like it is punching me in the gut voicing its objections." A ferocious cramp low in her belly shot through her, causing her to almost double over in pain, reinforcing her words.

"You need to sit down, Rachel. Come, here, set on this crate." Mary swiped a hand over the top of the wooden box to clear away any dust.

"*Danka.*" Rachel gratefully eased her body down, her hand automatically moving to press on the small of her back.

Mary started to pace fretfully up and down the space between several wagons, walking a circle around the box where Rachel sat. Her large hands continued to wring the apron she clutched.

Rachel could see how uncomfortable the girl was, how badly the events of the past few days had affected her. Although there was little light in the barn she could see the grimace on Mary's face, the pain in her eyes. She sought for words of comfort but few came to mind.

"I heard you've been asking questions, talking to that English woman deputy. Have you found out anything?"

Rachel flinched as another pain stabbed through her taut abdomen.

"Not really."

Mary stopped her pacing a few feet away from Rachel, eyeing her suspiciously. "You've been poking around enough you surely have heard something. Do you know if there are any 'people of interest' as they say."

Rachel shook her head. "I don't know anything. All I know is Naomi and Sarah were killed senselessly and only *Gott* knows why."

Then for an instant Rachel felt a flashback in time. An image of Mary K stopping her on the path to the restroom, how nervous she'd seemed. Could it be…no, it wasn't possible. Mary K couldn't be the killer.

At least, that's what she thought until she heard the other girl whisper hoarsely, "Naomi wasn't supposed to die."

CHAPTER 10 - GUT'S PROMISE

At first Rachel wasn't sure she heard right. She twisted her head around to look at the younger girl but Mary was standing with her back to her.

"No, Naomi shouldn't have died. And neither should have Sarah."

Mary whirled around then, fire blazing in her eyes.

"Sarah didn't deserve to live." She spat the words out as if they tasted like rotten eggs. "She was a sinner." Her hands furled and unfurled the apron she held, fingers working frantically.

Suspicion built in Rachel's mind, her heart rate picking up speed.

"But we're all sinners, Mary K." She kept her voice soft and soothing, struggling to keep it from trembling. "*Gott* loves us anyway, no matter what we've done. We just have to ask for his forgiveness and try to set our wrongs right."

The glow burning in Mary's eyes had gone from fiery to maniacal. She didn't even look like her, fury distorting her face. Her voice deepened, rough-edged and harsh.

"You don't understand. Sarah was interfering with *Gott's* work. She was bewitching Jacob Hochstetler. My Jacob. *Gott* promised him to me years ago."

Rachel slowly moved to stand up, groaning as another pain gripped her belly.

"So killing Naomi was an accident?"

A flash of lucidity came across the girl's face for a few seconds as she realized she had said too much…and then it was gone. Once again the glow of insanity burned in her eyes.

"I thought she was Sarah. I was sure of it so I followed her to the restroom. At first I was just going to talk to her, you know, just ask her to stay away from Jacob. But then, I saw her standing there washing her hands, and I knew." Mary nodded her head slowly. "I knew she had to die. That's when I took off my apron and snuck up behind her. I wrapped the strings around her neck and just started pulling…and pulling."

Rachel's eyes widened in horror as Mary grasped the strings of her apron and demonstrated how she strangled Naomi.

"She saw me in the mirror. She knew who I was." Her expression changed from fury to grief. "I saw her, too. I knew then that I had the wrong girl, but it was too late to stop. She would have told."

Rachel took a cautious step backwards. "So after you killed Naomi, you hid her in the handicap stall? Then you decided to try again to get to Sarah." Her shoulder bumped into the corner of a wagon making her pause. If she could just keep Mary K talking she might make it to the door, might get help for this girl with the damaged mind.

"Oh, she had to die then. She made me kill Naomi. She had to die."

"Did you know she would be making her egg deliveries that day?"

"Of course. She went the same day, same time every week. I just hid in the cornfield until I saw her coming than ran out into the road and screamed for help. I told her the killer was after me."

"So she stopped the buggy and told you to get in." Rachel used her toe to feel her way around the wagon bed, managing to get one step closer to the door.

"But instead of getting in I pulled her out. I jerked her down and threw her against a tree. She hit her head hard enough to stun her. After that, I killed her just like I did Naomi. Strangled her with my apron strings."

"Mary K, it wasn't your fault. You couldn't stop yourself." Rachel kept walking backwards but with each step back Mary took one towards her. "You have an illness, Mary. You need help. Let's get you some help."

"No!" The single word came out as a near scream, her foot stomping the concrete floor. She shook her head so hard the rest of her hair came tumbling down and swung around her face like writhing snakes. "No, it's not too late. I can still have Jacob if you don't tell what I told you. I can't let you tell."

Rachel whirled and ran for the door but her foot hooked on a wagon tongue and she stumbled to her hands and knees, concrete scraping tender flesh. Ignoring the pain she tried to get up but Mary was already there wrapping those deadly apron strings around her neck.

"I'm sorry, Rachel. I'm sorry. Now Sarah's making me kill you, too." Her strong hands pulled the strings tighter, cutting off Rachel's air supply.

Rachel fought like a wildcat, twisting and writhing in an attempt to free herself, her hands clawing at the constricting strands, scratching at Mary's clenched fists. Her vision was fading, lights beginning to twinkle behind her eyes. *Dear Gott* she silently prayed like she had never prayed before, *if I must die so be it, but please help me save my bobli.*

She gave up prying at Mary's hands and bent as far forward as possible trying to focus her blurring eyesight, searching for a weapon, any weapon.

Aaron, Aaron, I love you so much. Even now I can almost hear you calling my name.

There, a pile of bricks. If she could just reach one. Using her last bit of her energy she thrust herself forward and managed to grab an old red block. She swung the hand clutching her puny weapon straight up and felt it slam into Mary's forehead.

For just an instant the pressure loosened around her neck and Rachel dragged in a ragged breath before the strings tightened again. The last thing she saw before blackness took over was a red splotch of blood hit the floor like a splashing tear drop.

If this was heaven, it was mighty disappointing.

The thought flitted through Rachel's brain as her eyes fluttered open. Hammers instead of harps played in her ears, her throat felt raw and fiery, and she lay sprawled on her back on a rough, hard surface, pain racking her lower abdomen in a vice-like grip.

"Rachel, wake up. Can you hear me?" A strong arm lifted her shoulders, cradling her head against black clad trousers.

"Aar…Aaron, is that you?" She blinked furiously and the gray fog in front of her eyes began to clear. "Am I alive?"

"Yes, thank *Gott*, you are very much alive." His smile beamed, gratitude welling in his eyes as he helped her sit up. "Are you okay? Did she hurt you?

A wave of dizziness washed over her as she leaned against her husband. The memories came flooding back all at once, her eyes widening as she looked around.

"Mary K, where is she?"

Abby has her in the back of a patrol car. She was on top of you, choking you with her apron, when I found you."

"She killed Naomi." She nearly choked on the words. "And Sarah, too."

"I know, I know. But we need to think about you right now. Can you stand?"

"I...I think so." He helped her gently to her feet and Rachel realized the storm had ended and the sun was drying a newly washed world. And they weren't alone. She was surrounded by people. There was *Maemm*, and *Daett*. Her sisters and brothers stood close to their parents' sides and dozens of other people milled beyond the barn door, all with worried looks on their faces. So many *gut* people. She loved every one of them.

"How did you find me? I thought I was dead."

"When I couldn't locate you, I went looking. I saw your bonnet outside the door here."

Another pain wrapped around both sides of her belly and forced Rachel to bend over and groan, one arm wrapping protectively around her protruding stomach, the other clutching at Aaron's arm for support.

When at last she could straighten she looked solemnly into her husband's eyes.

"This mystery has been solved but now there is another one we must unravel."

Confusion skirted across Aaron's face. "What other mystery? We know Mary K is the killer. Case closed."

"Ah, but we're taking on a new case." A joyous smile wreathed her face "Only this unknown is one I can't wait to investigate. It's the mystery of childbirth and parenting…and I think it's starting right now."

It took a moment for her words to sink in but when they did Aaron's eyes grew wide, his eyebrows rising nearly to his hat brim.

"Now, Rachel? Are you sure?"

She nodded, a wondrous look painting her face as she turned her eyes upward.

"And see what Gott has sent to welcome our child? She raised a hand and pointed at the rainbow arching across the sky. "His promise that this story will have a happy ending."

Amish Investigation

SUSPICIOUS CONFESSIONS

CHAPTER 1

"You must be so excited about the wedding now it's almost here," said Hannah, her face lighting up with a smile.

Sarah nodded, "Yes, I am," she agreed. She knew she should be, and she was really trying her best to sound it.

She didn't look up from her needlework. She was worried her expression would give her away. It wasn't so much that she wasn't excited about the wedding. She was. It was the marriage she wasn't excited about.

"You don't sound excited," Hannah commented. She said it as statement, but Sarah knew it was more of a question. It wasn't a question she particularly wanted to answer, but she knew Hannah would dig until she got to the bottom of it.

Sarah put down her needlework with a sigh.

"Can you keep a secret?" she asked Hannah.

"Sure," Hannah said.

"Ok. I am excited about the wedding. Really I am. I know how much work has gone into it and I feel very honoured at how many people want me to be happy."

"But," prompted Hannah.

"But I don't want to marry Isaac," Sarah blurted out. She rushed to explain further before Hannah could start with the barrage of questions she would be sure to have.

"Isaac is a lovely man, I know that. He works hard, and his faith is admirable. I know it could have been a lot worse. And I really think he does love me. But the problem is, I don't love him. I like him, but I'm not in love with him. I'm not sure I ever will be, and I want my marriage to filled with love."

"Who is it?" asked Hannah.

"What do you mean?"

"Who is it that has your heart?"

That was one of the things Sarah loved about Hannah. She was extremely perceptive, and she spoke honestly, especially when there was just the two of them.

Sarah was torn. She badly needed someone to talk to and she really wanted to share her secret with Hannah, but she was afraid that Hannah would judge her.

At twenty-one, Hannah was a year older than Sarah, but Sarah felt she was so much wiser. Hannah had been lucky – her marriage had been arranged by her parents too, but she had fallen in love with the man they had chosen.

Sarah wished it had been that simple for her, but she felt guilty for having those thoughts, it made her feel like she was cheating on her true love to wish she could feel like that about someone else.

"His name is Colin," Sarah said, deciding she had to tell someone her secret. The guilt at the secret made her feel physically sick and she hoped sharing it would help.

"Colin?" Hannah exclaimed. "You mean he's not even Amish? Your parents would never agree to that."

"I know," sighed Sarah. "I know it could never work, but that doesn't stop me feeling this way. I was thinking of leaving the village to be with him. When I spoke to him about it, he refused. He said he could see how important my faith was to me and he didn't want to stand in the way of that in case I ended up resenting him. He said he would come here. He would convert so we could be together in a place that would make me happy."

"Well that's something I suppose. It shows how much he must really love you."

"I know. I tried to speak to my father about it but he wouldn't hear of it. He said the marriage was already arranged, and to let Isaac's family down now would damage his reputation too much."

"He has a point," said Hannah. "I would love to tell you to follow your heart Sarah, but we both know that's not how this works. God has a plan for all of us, and if He is showing that plan through your father, then you must follow it."

"I know, but it's hard."

"Often faith is hard, but you have to believe that there's a reason for all of this. Your father wants what's best for you and the family, and if he thinks that's Isaac, then it's not for you to argue. Isaac is a good man; you could have to endure much worse."

Sarah knew she was right, and she made a vow to herself that she would put all thoughts of Colin out of her mind. It wouldn't be easy, but if God was testing her, she intended to show that she had very strong faith and that she could do this.

"I'm just being stupid," she said. "I know I will marry Isaac, and I know in time I will forget about Colin and learn to love Isaac. You're right, my father does know what's best for me. I need to grow up and stop acting like a naughty child. I didn't mean to disrespect him."

"It's ok. This conversation is only between us; I promise you that. I don't think you intended to be disrespectful of your father's wishes."

Sarah picked her sewing back up again, pleased she had unburdened herself. She knew Hannah was right. It wasn't going to be easy, but she was going to force herself to look forward to the wedding and the life she and Isaac would share, no matter how difficult that would be. And she knew it be difficult.

The first thing she would have to do was to stop meeting Colin. She was meant to be meeting him that afternoon in his store and she made the decision not to go. She offered up a silent prayer that Colin would accept her decision and move on.

Forcing herself to sound enthusiastic, she started talking to Hannah about her upcoming wedding. She shared her nerves at saying her vows in front of the village elders.

Hannah laughed. "That one I can help with. Just focus on Isaac and pretend there's no one else in the room but you two."

Sarah thanked her for the advice and the girls chatted for a while about the beautiful feast her mother was planning for the reception. After a while, they fell into a comfortable silence as they both hurried to get through the pile of clothes they each had to repair.

CHAPTER 2

"Thanks Mrs Michaels," Colin said, handing the old lady her change and watching her leave the store.

He turned back to the shelves he was rearranging. He wanted the display to show Sarah's jam in pride of place. It was silly really, but it was the one thing he could do for her.

He sighed loudly as he moved the various jars and pots around.

"Too much like hard work?" asked Peter, his best friend and only employee.

They both laughed. "Women troubles." Colin told him.

"Tell me more," said Peter. "What's wrong, can't get any of them to go out with you?"

Normally Colin would have laughed at the ribbing, knowing it was meant in fun, but not today. Today, he just wanted to scream at how unfair it all was.

"I'll tell you, but you have to swear to me this conversation goes no further. If the wrong person found out about it, it could cause a lot of trouble."

"Ok," Peter agreed, serious now.

"Do you remember the little Amish girl, Sarah? She brings us these pots of jam to sell?"

Peter nodded, and Colin went on.

"The first time I spoke to her, I just knew there was something about her. I've never believed in love at first before, but something about that girl got me. I don't know if it was because she's so pure, or what, but from that first moment, I couldn't stop thinking about her.

"I used to buy her jams myself, then get word to her that we needed new stock. Eventually, I confessed to her what I was doing. I thought she might get upset, but I had to tell her. She didn't get upset, she smiled. And I knew then that she liked me too.

"We started seeing other in secret. She told me that she is promised to another man, one of her father's choosing, one she doesn't love. She started talking about leaving. I couldn't let her do that, it's obvious how important the Amish life is to her, so I said I would convert.

"She told me she would talk to her father about it, see if she could convince him to let us marry once I had converted. She was to meet me today and let me know what happened. She didn't come. I'm pretty sure that's my answer right there."

"That's some story," said Peter. "You sure know how to pick them don't you?"

Colin shrugged. "I can't help the way I feel. If I had a choice in the matter, of course I would choose to love someone available."

"So go to her. You know which village she lives in. Talk to her, make her see how you feel."

Colin shook his head. "I can't do that. It would force her to leave her village, her family, her whole life. I won't do that to her."

"But if her father saw how much she means to you, and you to her, maybe he would change his mind."

"It's not that simple," Colin told him. "The wedding is already planned. It would bring huge dishonour on her family if she was to back out now. Her father would never agree to it. It would just cause trouble for her."

"Her father doesn't sound like he cares what she wants. Maybe it would be best if she did leave."

"I thought all of this at first, but you have to understand that her father genuinely thinks what he has planned is best for her. The Amish community do things differently to us. Arranged marriages are the norm, and from what Sarah's told me, the man her father has chosen sounds like a decent enough man."

Peter considered this for a few minutes.

"So there's not really a lot you can do about it if you don't want to go to her."

"No, there isn't," Colin agreed.

"All you can do is try to move on. She's made her choice mate, and if you want to respect that, you're doing yourself no favours moping about over her. If she really loves you, she would want you to move on. That's surely why she hasn't shown up today. She's letting you go."

"I don't want her to let me go. I love her. But you're right. She's made her decision and I need to respect that. It's just going to take some time."

CHAPTER 3

Sarah felt a rush of worry go through her as she walked towards the house she shared with her parents. There was a police car parked outside it. The police only came here if they were bringing bad news. She quickened her step, worried her father had had a heart attack. Sarah and her mother were always telling him to slow down.

She pushed the front door open and went into the main room. Her mother and father were sitting at the table, two uniformed police officers sitting across from them.

The relief she felt at seeing her father sitting there alive and well was short lived when her mother spoke up.

"Come sit down love," said Miriam, and Sarah saw her eyes were red rimmed from crying. Her stomach whirling, she walked over and pulled out a chair.

"What's happened?" she asked, aiming her question at no one in particular.

She could feel her panic rising. Something really bad must have happened, and no one seemed in a rush to tell her what it was.

After a couple of minutes of silence, her father looked up at her, his face pale and his expression strained.

"Sarah," he started. "I'm so sorry, but you should hear this from me. It's Isaac."

He paused. Sarah knew what was coming, but she had to hear it, had to be sure.

"What about him?" she asked.

Miriam reached out and took Sarah's hand in hers. John, Sarah's father, continued.

"He was murdered," he said simply.

Sarah didn't what to say, what to feel. Her head was spinning dizzily. She felt a hundred different emotions flood through her at once. Disbelief – who would want to hurt Isaac? Horror at the thought of something like this touching their peaceful community. Fear at what this meant for her. And although she was loathe to admit it, a tiny part of her felt relieved that the marriage wouldn't go ahead.

"Are you ok?" asked Miriam, and Sarah realised a couple of minutes had gone past without her speaking.

"I, I don't know," she answered honestly.

The female officer spoke up. "Miss Fisher, we need to ask you a couple of questions. If you need some time we can come back later, but the sooner we get this information, the sooner we can start trying to catch whoever did this."

Steeling herself, Sarah took a deep breath. What she was about to say would change everything. It would bring shame on her parents, she would be reviled by her community, but she knew she had to do it. She couldn't live with herself if she didn't tell the truth. How could she sit and lie before God?

She looked the female officer directly in the eye. "It was me. I killed him," she said simply.

"Nonsense," bellowed John, standing up so quickly his chair fell to the floor behind him. Sarah winced at the bang. "She's upset. She doesn't know what she's saying."

The male officer, who so far hadn't spoken now addressed John.

"Calm down sir. We'll get to the bottom of this, but I'm afraid we will be arresting your daughter."

"You can't do that, please," said Miriam quietly, clutching Sarah's hand so tightly her knuckles where white.

"It's ok mother," said Sarah before either of the officers had a chance to respond. She turned to the officers. "What happens now?"

She felt strangely calm, relieved of the burden of her guilty secret, and she was ready to face the consequences of what she had done.

The female officer produced a set of handcuffs. Sarah prised her mother's fingers from her hand, tears running freely down her face. "I'm sorry," she said to her parents.

She held her hands out in front of her and the female officer cuffed her wrists. "Sarah Fisher," she said. "I'm arresting you on suspicion of the murder of Isaac Beiler. You don't have to say anything, but anything you do say can be used against you later in court. You have the right to an attorney."

The officers led Sarah towards the door. She looked back to get one last look at her home, her parents. They stood side by side, her father's arm placed protectively around her mother's shoulders, his expression cold and stoic. Her mother was openly crying now, and Sarah suspected her father's arm was as much to hold her mother back as it was to offer comfort.

"I'm sorry," she said again as the door closed behind her.

* * *

THE CELL DOOR was slid open. "Sarah Fisher," said the guard.

She stood up. "That's me," she said.

"This way," he instructed.

She left the cell and followed him. "Where are you taking me?" she asked.

"I do the asking around here. You go where you're told."

Sarah bit her lip. She was used to not asking questions, following instructions. This wasn't all that new to her and she knew she could survive this part. It was what awaited her back at her cell that worried her. The other woman here where worldly. They understood how the system worked, and they seemed to have no fear.

Sarah was terrified. She hadn't expected to be locked up with criminals. She knew in hindsight that was stupid.

Why wouldn't she be locked up with criminals, she was one now. A terrible one.

Sarah followed the guard down a brightly lit corridor, and into what looked like a store room.

"Fisher," he said simply, announcing her arrival, propelling her into the centre of the room where a female guard waited.

The female guard looked her up and down and selected an orange jumpsuit and a pair of white plimsolls that looked like they had seen better days.

"Strip," she commanded. "Then put your clothes in there." She pointed to a large container.

Sarah looked around her for a place to change.

"No place to be shy here," the guard said.

Sarah knew if she argued, she'd be in even more trouble. With trembling fingers, she removed her clothes. She stood naked, cold, covering herself as best she could with her arms.

The guard indicated the container where she had placed her clothes. "This it?" she asked. No other possessions?"

"That's it," Sarah confirmed.

The guard approached her. "Arms out to the sides, legs spread," she said.

Sarah shook her head, tears rolling down her cheeks. "I'm sorry, I can't do this," she spluttered out.

The guard's expression softened slightly. "Look, I know you're not used to this kind of thing, I'll make it as easy possible if you co-operate. I'm not out to embarrass you, I'm just doing what has to be done. We can do this the easy way, or I can call for back up, tell them you're not co-operating, and the search will be a forced one. It won't be pleasant."

Sarah noticed her world weary tone and decided she wasn't bluffing. Slowly, she raised her arms and moved her legs apart. She felt herself blushing with shame.

The guard patted her down, checking in her arm pits and under her breasts, her fingers groping in Sarah's hair. "All clear," she said. "Squat and cough."

"What?" said Sarah, sure she'd heard wrongly. "What do you think would be in there?"

Her surprise registered with the guard, who realised it was a genuine question. "You'd be surprised love."

She did as she was told, more hot tears of shame running down her face.

She stood back up and followed the guard's instructions to put the uniform on. The guard led her to a table and took her finger prints, then took her photograph.

"Let's go," she said, leading Sarah back through the door she had entered through. She led her back towards her cell, but then she turned off surprising Sarah.

"Am I being moved?" asked Sarah, surprised.

"You'll be joining gen pop in a little while, but first, your attorney's in there," she nodded towards a door.

Seeing Sarah's blank expression, she elaborated. "Gen pop is general population. Now you've been booked in, you'll go in the main prison until your hearing date. Your attorney will try and get you bail."

"I don't have an attorney," said Sarah, still struggling to process the fact she was going into real prison.

"Sure you do. State appoints one," the guard opened the door and Sarah stepped into a small white room. The only furniture was a table, bolted to the floor, and two flimsy plastic chairs. A woman sat in one of the chairs.

"Thank you. You can leave us alone now," the woman said to the guard, who closed and locked the door behind her.

"Sit down," the woman said, nodding towards the other chair. "I'm Molly Carlisle, your defence lawyer. The first thing I'm going to do is file a motion to have your confession thrown out. I think I can persuade the judge that it was panic that made you blurt that out. That in your grief you weren't thinking straight."

"No," said Sarah. "That's not true. I did it."

Molly looked at Sarah for a few minutes.

"I don't know what's going on here, but I know a killer when I see one, and I'd be willing to bet my last dollar that you're not one. It's my job to represent you Sarah, and I am going to get that confession thrown out. Do we understand each other."

Sarah nodded. "I understand what you're saying, but you have to understand that I'm not going to lie in court. I did this, and I won't say otherwise."

"Then we'll compromise," said Molly. "Just sit quietly and don't say anything at all. Take care, I'll be seeing you soon."

She stood and banged on the door. It was unlocked quickly, and Molly was gone. Sarah was led back away to her new cell.

Molly sat in her car thinking. She didn't know why that girl was willing to confess to a murder Molly didn't believe for a second she had committed, but she intended to find out. Whoever she was covering for, whoever she was afraid of, Molly was determined to see justice was done. That girl had touched something in Molly and she knew she wouldn't rest until she reached the truth.

CHAPTER 4

"It's lovely here," said Gemma, looking around her at the contemporary décor of the restaurant. "I hope the food is as good as the rest of it."

"It is," Colin smiled.

He looked across at Gemma. She was beautiful, with long dark curls, and olive skin. She wore a red dress that showed off her ample cleavage, something Sarah would never be able to do. He found himself comparing the two women in his mind, and he decided he liked the modest way Sarah dressed. It was simple, classy.

He had known for a while that Gemma liked him, but he had never been in a position to go on a date with her.

He had finally asked her out, and here they were on their first date.

Colin watched as Gemma took a drink of her wine, her throat moving slightly as she swallowed. He had to admit that the view was a good one. She really was attractive. But she wasn't Sarah.

Colin kicked himself mentally. He had to accept that his relationship with Sarah was over. It would never have worked. He had been fooling himself all those months thinking it ever could have worked. They were from different worlds, worlds that would never meet successfully.

Colin wondered if he had done the right thing asking Gemma out, He knew Peter was right, he had to try and move on, but he worried it was too soon. He felt like he was using Gemma, and it wasn't fair on her. He had to accept that no one would live up to Sarah in his mind, but he had to find someone who would come a pretty close second.

"Who is she?" Gemma asked with a small smile.

"Huh?"

"The girl that's on your mind."

"I don't know what you mean," Colin lied.

"Sure you do," said Gemma. "You've never been interested in me before, so I'm figuring you just broke up with someone, and I'm the rebound girl. She's obviously still on your mind. You've barely said two words since you picked me up and you're squirming around in your seat like you're waiting for me to attack you or something."

"I was with a girl, but it's over now. She's not on my mind, it will never work out between us. I'm just quiet because I'm nervous."

Colin still felt guilty, of course Sarah was on his mind, but it was only a half lie.

Gemma's smile widened. "You don't have to be nervous with me, I promise I don't bite."

Colin laughed. He made a conscious effort to push all thoughts of Sarah out of his mind. He would enjoy this evening with Gemma if it killed him. He was hopeful that in time, Gemma would grow on him and he would fall for her in the way he had fallen for Sarah.

Hopeful yes, but he wasn't convinced it would happen. Not by a long shot. Not that there was anything wrong with Gemma, he just felt that no one could take Sarah's place in his heart.

CHAPTER 5

Molly entered the prison, armed with her folder full of findings. She was itching to talk to Sarah about what she had discovered. She was pretty sure she had stumbled on the person Sarah was so afraid of. The person she was willing to confess for. Molly thought maybe he had threatened her family.

She was taken to the same small room as the last time she had met with Sarah, and she sat down to wait for Sarah to be brought to her.

She read through her notes again, even though she knew them off by heart.

The door opened, and Sarah was ushered in. She sat down across from Molly.

Molly waited until the guard who had escorted her had left and locked the door.

"How's it going?" she asked. Sarah didn't look too bad. She was pale, paler than before, but no visible bruising which she took as a good sign.

Sarah shrugged. "I keep to myself and don't bother anyone, and so far, they all seem happy enough to ignore me."

Molly heard the tremor in her voice. Sarah knew what she knew – they wouldn't leave her alone forever, only until they found something she could be useful for, or she looked the wrong way at the wrong person on the wrong day. Prison was no place for someone like Sarah.

"Sarah, you don't have to be afraid to tell me the truth," Molly started. "If someone is threatening you or your family, there's witness protection schemes. We can get you on one, change your identity and keep you safe."

"No one is threatening me," said Sarah.

"Are you sure?" Molly asked. Something in Sarah's quiet demeanour convinced Molly she was telling the truth, but she had to be sure.

"I'm sure," Sarah repeated. "Why would someone be threatening me?"

Molly glanced down at her notes again, more for effect than to refresh her memory.

"Sarah, I've been looking into this. The police are happy to let it drop. They have a confession, they don't need to dig any further, but I do. I refuse to allow you to stay in prison for a crime you didn't commit. I've found about the debt."

"Debt?"

"The money Isaac owed to Marcus Slade. I understand why you're frightened but it's ok. What we discuss here is confidential."

"I don't know what you're talking about. What debt? Who's this Marcus man?"

Molly didn't believe Sarah to be so good an actress that she could fool her. Her confusion was real. She didn't know about the money.

"Sarah, a couple of months before Isaac was killed, he borrowed in excess of $20,000 from Marcus Slade. Slade isn't a nice man. When it came time to repay the money, Isaac didn't have it. I believe that is why he was killed."

Sarah didn't respond, and Molly left the silence to grow.

Sarah's head was reeling again. The debt explained a lot. It explained how Isaac had been able to extend the farm when he seemed to never have any money, and it explained why he had been so on edge the last few weeks. He had known it was getting to be time to pay the debt back and that he didn't have the money anymore. He would have had no one to turn to for help, it was frowned upon to borrow outside money, especially from someone like the man Molly was describing.

"I didn't know any of this. I was going to marry Isaac and it turns out I didn't know him at all," Sarah said finally, breaking the silence.

"In light of this, I'm confident we can have you out of here in a few weeks," Molly said, expecting Sarah to be pleased.

"No," Sarah shook her head emphatically. "No. I'm responsible for this. I don't deserve to be free."

"Sarah, you are not responsible for this," Molly said gently. "Even if he got the money for you, you didn't kill him."

"He didn't get the money for me. He extended his farm. He needed a new barn."

"Then why are you insisting this is your fault?"

"You wouldn't understand."

"Make me understand. I can't help you if you won't talk to me."

"That's what you don't understand. I don't want your help. I want to accept my punishment and make things right."

After that, Sarah clammed up, refusing to respond to any more of Molly's questions. Molly gave up after a while and knocked on the door to be released. As she left, she turned back to Sarah. "This isn't over," she told her.

CHAPTER 6

Molly opened the gate to the Fisher residence. She felt a little nervous. She had never really dealt with Amish families before and she wasn't sure how they would react to having an uninvited lawyer turn up on their doorstep. She just hoped that they would see she was looking out for their daughter.

She walked up the path and knocked gently on the door. Within minutes, a man opened the door.

"Yes?" he enquired.

"Hi Mr Fisher, I'm Molly Carlisle, I'm your daughter's attorney. I wondered if I could come in and talk to you and your wife about your daughter's confession?"

"I have nothing to say to you," John said, pushing the door closed. "It's people like you who got her into this mess."

Molly reached out a hand to stop it. "Please," she said. "I'm on your daughter's side here."

"With respect miss, please remove your hand from my door."

Molly did. She could sense she would get nothing from John. He didn't trust the system, and she could hardly blame in light of recent events. Molly got back in her car and sat thinking, drumming her fingers on the steering wheel. She wasn't ready to give up just yet, but she was stumped as to where she should go next.

She got back out of the car and started walking along the block. She had spotted a small tea shop and she'd decided to pop in and ask around, see if anyone there knew who Sarah was close to.

As she walked along, she heard footsteps running up behind her.

"Wait," a voice panted. She turned around and saw a middle aged woman running towards her gasping for breath.

"Are you ok?" she asked, as the red-cheeked woman caught up to her.

"Yes," panted the woman. "I don't have much time. My husband thinks I've gone to the neighbours to borrow a cup of flour. I have to go and get some so he doesn't know I lied. I don't like lying to him, but it had to be done. How is she?"

With the last question, Molly released who the woman was. Sarah's mother.

"She's ok Mrs Fisher. She's holding up well, keeping herself to herself."

"She didn't kill anyone. I don't care what she says, my daughter just isn't capable of murder."

"For what it's worth, I agree with you. I think I know who did, and it definitely wasn't your daughter. The trouble is, she won't retract her confession, and the police consider the case closed. I'm confident I can get it re-opened when I present my findings, but I'm concerned about why Sarah is lying about this. If I go in too soon, I could be putting her in danger."

Miriam looked down at her shoes, her hands flitted about each other nervously. Molly let her have a moment to get her thoughts straight. Just when Molly thought she wasn't going to say anything, she did.

"Will you tell her I'm sorry I haven't been to visit? Her father thinks we should distant ourselves from this a bit until the dust settles, but I miss her every day."

Molly had to bite her tongue. She wanted to shake the woman, make her see she could go and see her daughter on her own. She reminded herself that they do things differently here, and that she had to respect their beliefs, especially if she wanted Mrs Fisher to cooperate.

"I will," she said. "Mrs Fisher, can you think of a reason, any reason at all, why your daughter would confess to this?"

"Honestly, I've thought about nothing else since she was arrested, and I keep coming up blank. Sarah was acting strange, distant, before this happened. I tried to talk to her about what was wrong, but she kept telling me I imagining things, or that she was nervous about the wedding. I didn't believe her then and I don't now, but I'm still stumped as to what's going on. If anyone would know, it would be Hannah."

"Who's Hannah?"

"Sarah's best friend. You'll find her over in the orchard today picking fruit." She turned Molly a little to her left. "Just down there, you can't miss it. Now, I really have to go, my husband will be getting suspicious. Please help my Sarah."

"Thank you Mrs Fisher. I will get your daughter out of there, I promise."

Sometimes, you just have to tell people what they want to hear, but this time, Molly meant it. She wouldn't rest until Sarah Fisher was back home where she belonged. Miriam following her like that had furthered her resolve. To defy her husband and risk the retribution of that showed how much Miriam loved her daughter.

She followed the path that Miriam had pointed out to her. It didn't take long until she came across a small wooden gate with a sign reading "The Orchard". Molly smiled to herself, she had thought Miriam was holding back, purposely not telling her who the orchard belonged to. Now it became apparent why she had referred to it that way.

She opened the gate and made her way inside. She spotted who she was looking for straight away, or at least she assumed the small blonde girl was Hannah.

"Hannah?" she asked when she had closed the distance enough to be heard.

The girl nodded.

"Have you got five minutes to chat?" Molly asked.

Hannah's face instantly changed one of suspicion.

"Are you a journalist?" she asked.

"No," Molly said, "but I guess that means the press have been bothering you. My name's Molly, I'm Sarah's attorney. I'm trying to help her."

Hannah still eyed her with suspicion.

"Sarah's mother told me where to find you. She took a big risk talking to me against her husband's wishes. Please don't let that be in vain."

Hannah's face relaxed. If Mrs Fisher had talked to Molly, so could she.

"Yes, Sarah's father has washed his hands of her altogether. He was part of the reason she was so unhappy."

"Why was she so unhappy?" asked Molly.

"Because her father was making her marry Isaac. She made her peace with it, but he didn't make her happy."

Molly didn't like the sound of that. It sounded awfully like a motive.

"Hannah, do you believe your friend had anything to do with Isaac's murder?"

Hannah shook her head vigorously. "No. I really don't. Sarah would never do that. She has such a deep faith; she wouldn't go against everything she believed in like that. Usually growing up, we struggle with our faith and its restrictions. It's almost a rite of passage for Amish kids, but Sarah never did.

"That's why she agreed to go ahead with the wedding, because her faith gave her reason to believe that this was the plan for her."

"Did Isaac hurt Sarah?" asked Molly, confused as to why Sarah was so adamant she didn't want to marry him.

"No, of course not. Isaac was a good man. He really loved Sarah."

"So why was she so against marrying him?"

"I'm sorry. I can't say. Sarah would never forgive me."

"Please Hannah. This could be the difference between Sarah being free, or spending her life in prison for a crime she didn't commit. Please help me to understand what's happening here. I swear I won't tell her any of what we speak about."

Hannah was silent for a second, then Molly saw her face change. Her eyes filled with determination, and her mouth set in a straight line.

"Sarah didn't want to marry Isaac because she didn't love him. She loved someone else, someone outside the faith. She went to her father, told him that the man she loved was willing to convert to the faith. She begged him to reconsider her engagement, but he said it was too late. It would bring too much shame on the family."

"Who is the man?"

"All I know is his name's Colin and he works in a small store in the next village. He buys Sarah's family's jams. That's how they met."

"Thank you Hannah." Molly turned to leave.

"Molly?" Hannah called after her.

"Yeah."

"Please don't tell him who told you this if you go to see him."

"I won't," Molly promised.

Back in her car and driving to the next village, Molly tried again to make sense of everything she had heard so far.

What she had found out today gave Sarah a perfect motive, but she still knew in her heart of hearts that Sarah wasn't the guilty party. She just had to find a way to prove it.

She hoped Colin would be able to shed some light on the situation. Maybe it was him? With Isaac out of the way, he maybe thought that they could be together, and Sarah had confessed to protect him. No, she told herself, his debts got him killed. Not Colin and not Sarah.

Molly was getting more frustrated every day with this case. She felt like every time she got a question answered, it raised two more.

Molly reached the village Hannah had sent her to and drove through to the centre, hopeful that's where she would find the stores. She soon came upon a small row of stores. She parked her car and walked along the street.

Some of the stores where easy to rule out – there was a small hardware store and a used bookstore, but a lot of them appeared to sell a mixture of things. Molly narrowed it down to five stores to begin with.

She entered the first and had a look around. She couldn't spot any home-made jam so she decided this couldn't be the place. As she went to leave, the door behind the counter opened and a woman stepped through.

"Can I help you?" she asked with a smile.

"Maybe," said Molly, hoping this was one of those places where everyone knew each other. "I'm looking for Colin? I don't know his surname, but I've been told he has a shop on this street."

"Oh, Colin. He's two doors down honey. Tell him I said hi."

"Thank you."

Molly entered Colin's store and had a quick look about. She spotted the home-made jams straight away, they had pride of place on Colin's shelves. She smiled to herself. This was the place alright.

A man she presumed to be Colin stood behind the counter chatting to the customer he was serving. Molly could see why Sarah liked him. He had an easy charm about him.

When he finished serving his customer and she had left the store, Molly approached the counter.

"Hi. Colin?" she asked even though she already knew the answer.

He nodded.

"Can I ask you a few questions about your relationship with Sarah Fisher?"

"I don't know what you're talking about," he said, the smile staying on his face but leaving his eyes.

"I think you do."

"Look, she sells me jam, sometimes chutney. That's it. We pass the time of day together. That's it. Please leave now."

"I'm not a cop," Molly said, sensing he had been questioned a few times. Maybe the police weren't calling this closed just yet. It sounded like they had had a similar theory to her. But how had they known about him?

"A cop? Why would I think you were a cop?"

Molly cringed. He hadn't heard about Sarah. Now she was going to have to tell him. But first, she wanted to get to the bottom of who he had thought she was. Before she had a chance to continue, Colin solved the problem of who he thought she was.

"Look, I know there was some rumours in the village that Sarah and I shared more than just jam if you know what I mean. It's simply not true. Sarah is an honourable woman who is engaged to another man and I respect that as does she. So if you're trying to make trouble for her, you're wasting your time."

Now Molly understood. Rumours spread quickly in a small village like this.

"Actually, I'm trying to help Sarah. This may come as a shock to you Colin, you might want to sit down."

He frowned at her. "What's happened to her?" He didn't sit down.

"Isaac Beiler was murdered two weeks ago. Sarah has confessed to the crime. I'm her attorney, and her confession doesn't wash with me. I have good reason to believe she didn't commit any crime, and I'm trying to get to the bottom of why she would make a false confession."

Upon hearing that, Colin did sit down. He sat down hard, his face strained. He fought to get control of his emotions.

"You mean Sarah is in jail?" he asked, the shock evident on his face and in his voice.

Molly nodded sadly. "Can you think of any reason why she would make a false confession?"

"No," Colin said, "I'm completely stumped. It just isn't something she would do. She prides herself on her honesty. Do you think she's being forced into it?"

"Maybe," Molly said. She went on. "Colin, no one except me visits her. Her father won't allow it. Do you think you could visit her? I'm sure she'd love to see you and maybe she'll open up to you."

Colin shook his head.

"No. I'm sorry, but I can't do that. Me and Sarah, it's over, I need to move on and so does she. I couldn't bear to see her again and drag up all those old feelings."

Molly knew better than to try and persuade him. He didn't owe her anything, and if he didn't want to help Sarah, then there was nothing she would be able to say to change his mind.

She handed him her card. "If you change your mind, or you think of anything at all that could help, give me a call."

CHAPTER 7

Colin sat on his settee watching a re-run of an old black and white movie. Actually, he wasn't watching it. He was just staring in its direction as his head span with thoughts of Sarah. His Sarah. How had it come to this?

He could picture her locked in a cell – lost, afraid. He wanted nothing more than to go to her, but he was afraid of what she would think. Would she think now Isaac was out of the way he was trying to swoop in? If she did think that, would it make her happy rather than angry?

There was so much he didn't know.

The one thing he did know, and probably had known since the moment Molly told him what was happening, is that he couldn't abandon Sarah, not now. Not when she needed him the most.

He picked up Molly's card from his coffee table where he had put it upon returning home. He turned it round and round, running his thumb over it, thinking.

He pulled his cell out and dialled.

"Hello."

"Hi Gemma, it's Colin."

"Oh, hi Colin. I didn't expect hearing from you," she said.

"I know. I don't know why I called. I'm sorry."

"It's ok. When I said we should still be friends, I meant it. We only went on one date, it's hardly a reason to never speak again. It sounds like you really need a friend."

"You have no idea how true that is right now."

"Does it have something to do with a certain pretty little lady who was looking for you this afternoon?"

"Yes, but not how you think. Remember on our date I told you about being in love with someone else but I needed to move on because it could never work? Well maybe now it can work. Or maybe it still can't, I don't know. What I do know is she needs me and I have to go to her. That woman who came looking for me today, she was Sarah's lawyer. I have to go talk to Sarah, find out what's going on, try and help her."

"So, let me get this straight. The woman you're hung up on is Sarah Fisher. The Amish girl who confessed to murdering her fiancé? Did she do it so you two could be together?"

"No." It came out louder than Colin had intended and he started over. "No. Nothing like that. She isn't capable of murder. Her lawyer thinks she knows who actually did it, but she can't work out why Sarah made a false confession. I don't know what to do. I feel so helpless."

"Let me ask you one question. I need a yes or no answer. No theatrics because I'm not judging, I'm just asking."

"Go on."

"If the lawyer is wrong, and Sarah did kill her fiancé, would you still want to go to her?"

"Yes," Colin said without hesitation.

"There's your answer Colin. Now go get her."

This time, Colin did dial Molly's number. She answered on the second ring, a note of irritation in her voice.

"I'm sorry, is this a bad time? I can call back."

"No. Wait. Is that you Colin?"

"Yes. I'll do it. I'll go visit her."

"It's too late. She was released an hour ago. New forensic evidence came to light that proved who the killer was. It wasn't Sarah, it was one of the loan shark's trained goons like I thought."

"That's fantastic news. Why don't you sound happy?"

"Because even now, with the bad guy locked up and her free, Sarah is still insisting she is guilty. I guess she touched me a little more than a client should. I'm worried about her."

CHAPTER 8

"How did you sleep," asked Miriam as Sarah entered the kitchen the morning after she had been released.

"Very well thank you," she replied.

"Sarah," John said. "I want you to understand that everything I have done has been about protecting the reputation of our family, you included."

Sarah knew how hard it must have been for her father to say that to her. It was the closest he could come to apologising and in her heart, she knew he was trying to do the right thing by them all.

"It's ok father, I understand," she said with a smile. "Let's not talk about it anymore. I just want things to go back to how they were."

Her father gave a curt nod. He was a man of few words.

"I have to go and meet Hannah," Sarah said. "I promised to help her gather the last of the fruit from the orchard."

"Ok dear," her mother replied.

With her heart lighter than it had been since that fateful time when the police came to her house, Sarah half skipped to meet up with Hannah.

"Sarah," Hannah exclaimed with delight when she spotted her. "What are doing here? How long have you been home?"

"I got home last night. Where else would I be? I promised to help you gather the fruit and here I am."

"A lot has changed since then."

"Not really. It was just something that had to happen. I'm back now and I'm putting the past behind me. I'm ready more than ever to trust in both God and my father to allow me to make the right choices."

"You seem different. Lighter somehow."

"I guess I am. I feel freer than ever Hannah. God has shown me the way."

Happy for her friend, Hannah threw her arms around Sarah. "It's great to have you back."

"It's great to be back. Now let's get down to work."

* * *

COLIN KNOCKED ON THE DOOR. He straightened his tie as he waited for it to be answered.

"Yes?" John said as he opened the door and looked Colin up and down.

"Mr Fisher, I need to talk to you. Please hear me out, and if at the end of the conversation, you think I'm crazy, or that what I'm about to say is a bad idea, then I'll walk away and never look back. You have my word on that. Please."

"What?" John said, totally lost as to who this man was and what he wanted from him.

"Let him in," said Miriam, coming up behind John.

"You know this man?"

"Yes. It's Colin from the next village. He buys our jams. And I think he has our daughter's heart."

Both Colin and John looked shocked.

"I'm right aren't I?" Miriam asked Colin. "You're the one she wanted to marry. She was always so happy when she came back from the store, always had an extra bounce in her step."

Colin nodded mutely. John stood back and allowed him in, not sure what else to do.

"Thank you Mr Fisher, Mrs Fisher," Colin said as he sat in the seat Miriam pointed to.

"Let's hear it then," said John.

"I love your daughter. And I know she loves me. I assure you, nothing untoward has happened between us, and when you refused your permission for us to be together, Sarah stayed away. I tried to move on, but I can't stop thinking about her. I'm here to ask you, no to beg you, to let me marry your daughter. I will convert to Amish and I promise I will work hard and spend every day of the rest of my life making your daughter happy."

John paused to consider the words. "It wouldn't be easy for you, coming here and changing your entire lifestyle."

"I understand that, but I will do it. That's how much Sarah means to me."

"You can never truly convert, but you can live here in the village, as long as you follow the rules and traditions and you must observe the faith we live by. It's been done before."

"Does that mean I have your blessing to marry you daughter Mr Fisher?"

"Yes," John said. He knew it would be next to impossible to find a good marriage for her after recent events, and Colin seemed like a decent young man. If he allowed himself to be really honest, he felt he owed Sarah the chance to be happy. He had had many a sleepless night wondering if everything would have turned out differently if he just said yes to Sarah's request to call off her wedding. Isaac would still be gone, but his daughter, the light of his life wouldn't have been to prison, and he wouldn't have had to make the soul destroying decision of cutting her off.

"Mrs Fisher?" Colin said.

"I just want Sarah to be happy, so yes. And its Miriam now, and he's John."

"Thank you. You have no idea how much this means to me. I promise to be the best husband I can be to Sarah."

"You should leave now. Come back this evening when Sarah will be home, after I tell her what's happening."

Colin stood, and as he went to thank them again, the front door opened and in walked Sarah.

"Colin," she said, stopping in her tracks.

"Sarah," he said back.

"We'll let you two talk for a minute," said Miriam, standing and pulling John to his feet and towards the back door.

"Not a word of what we spoke about," John warned as he left.

"What are you doing here?" asked Sarah.

"I had some business to take care of with your father. How are you Sarah."

"Good. How are you?"

"Ok, except for missing you every single day. Sarah I'm so sorry I wasn't there when you needed me. I didn't hear until the day before you were released."

"It's ok," she shrugged.

"What happened Sarah, why did you confess to a crime you didn't commit?"

"You wouldn't understand. Let's just say that sometimes, the man who actually pulls the trigger is just a tool being used by someone higher up."

"Sarah, I love you. Nothing will change that. Make me understand why you think you were somehow responsible for what happened to Isaac."

Sarah's eyes filled with tears. She gave a small nod and looked him in the face.

"Night after night, I laid awake thinking about you. Dreaming of what our lives would be like together. The little store we would run, or the farm. How we would cuddle in front of the open fire on cold nights. Our little children running around in the sunshine laughing. How happy we would be.

"There was only one thing stopping us, and that was Isaac. Night after night I prayed that he would just disappear. And then he did. God answered my prayers, but I felt terrible, like I had blasphemed.

"So you see, the man who pulled the trigger, he was just a tool, sent to answer my wishes. I didn't mean it to turn out like that though Colin. I wouldn't have wished that on Isaac, he was a good man, he just wasn't you.

"I knew I had to be punished for what I had done, so I didn't try to shift the blame. I owned up and I was punished. I spent hours in silent prayer, asking for God's forgiveness. And then I was freed. I think God punished me enough, and now I have been forgiven."

She was openly crying now, and it broke Colin's heart. He couldn't imagine how she must have been feeling. Locked up away from her family and friends with such a huge burden on her small shoulders, and no one to turn to for comfort.

"Oh, Sarah," he said, going to her and pulling her into a tight embrace as she cried. She held him tightly for a second then stepped back.

"Sarah, you know deep down that this isn't how it works don't you? You are not to blame for Isaac's murder. Isaac borrowed money off a bad man, and that is why he ended up murdered, not because of you.

"I think it's true that God had a plan for you Sarah, but I don't think that plan was to torture yourself with guilty feelings. I think God's plan was for us to be together all along, but it's true that he works in mysterious ways.

"I believe this was His way of testing our love for one another."

"Do you really think so?"

Colin nodded. "I do. I think God could see your good intentions, and that you just wanted to follow your heart. God promotes love, how could he turn his back on a girl that was in love?"

"Maybe you're right. Maybe that's why I feel so free. Not because my guilt has been lifted, but because I am free to love you again."

Her face fell.

"Except my father will never agree to this."

At that moment, John, who had been listening at the back door, came back into the house followed by Miriam.

"By not breaking your promise, you have proved trustworthy Colin. Now you and me, we need to talk."

Colin followed John into the other room.

Miriam remained with Sarah, fussing over her and giving her a cup of hot tea. She was so happy to have her daughter back.

"Colin's a nice man," Miriam said. "He makes you happy."

"He does," Sarah smiled at the mention of his name. The smile faltered. "But I've accepted my fate. My father knows best and I will do what he wishes."

Miriam wished she could tell Sarah the news, but it wasn't her place to do so. Instead, she squeezed Sarah's hand and said simply "Trust in the Lord Sarah."

CHAPTER 9

John was satisfied he given Colin enough of a pep talk. He'd warned him about hurting Sarah and bringing disrepute on the family. He'd talked to him about the Amish belief system and their way of life, in particular life in this village.

Colin had readily agreed. Before suggesting to Sarah that he convert, he had done enough research to know roughly what the Amish life entailed, and he knew with Sarah by his side, he could live anywhere by any set of rules.

By the end of his research, and even more so by the end of his talk with John, he found himself looking forward to a simpler way of life. A life that valued love, honesty and hard work over material possessions. A life that valued family over boozy nights out. It sounded almost too good to be true, yet here he was being accepted into the way of life, and being welcomed into his new family.

"I think it's about time you went and asked Sarah to marry you," John said, clapping Colin on the back.

The two men re-joined Miriam and Sarah in the main room. John went and sat beside Miriam.

Colin walked over to Sarah and got down on one knee before her.

"Sarah. I've loved you from the very first moment I saw you, and nothing would make me happier than to spend the rest of my life with you. I promise I will strive every day to make you happy, and I will love you until my dying breath and beyond.

"I always pictured doing this with a ring, but as your community have taught me, we don't need a ring to show our love for each other. We just need each other.

"Would you do me the huge honour of agreeing to be my wife?"

Sarah's eyes overflowed again, this time with joy. She looked over to where John sat, and he gave a barely discernible nod. She had his permission.

Half laughing, half crying, Sarah nodded enthusiastically. "Yes," she exclaimed. "Nothing would make me happier."

Colin stood and pulled Sarah gently to her feet. He kissed the back of her hand. "Then with God as my witness, I pledge myself to you Sarah Fisher. I love you."

"I love you too."

Sarah had never been happier than she was right now. She looked over at her parents. Her mother was wet eyed and smiling, and her father looked genuinely happy too. He had his arm around her mother, and this time, Sarah was sure it was a declaration of love.

After all, John had worked hard to persuade Sarah's grandfather, Miriam's father, that he was right for her. And now, he had been the one to make Sarah's dream come true. Her mother had been right. She just had to trust in the Lord and everything would work out. She was the living proof of that.

She thought she might burst with happiness; she couldn't speak for the tears of joy still pouring out of her.

"No time for standing around crying," said John laughing. "We've got a wedding to organise."

Amish Investigation

Amish Investigation

HOME FIRES BURNING

Amish Investigation

CHAPTER 1 - FIRE IN THE SKY

The barn raising had gone well. The new building was being erected to replace one destroyed by an unexplained fire and was now nearly complete. Katie Bontrager smiled as she eyed the fresh construction. Much progress had been made. This was *gut*. Soon the Gruber farm could return to normal.

Now it was time to feed the men who worked so hard and accomplished so much today. No one could deny that Amish men labored well together. They worked as a team, just as the Amish women worked together to prepare a hearty dinner to reward the men's efforts and keep track of the multitude of children running about.

The dinner would take place in the new barn. Tables were pulled into place and weighted down with hams, roast chickens, and beef and noodles. Potato salads, macaroni salads, and bean salads added to the feast accompanied by fresh baked yeast rolls, zucchini bread, and bowls of macaroni and cheese and fluffy potatoes. The last of this summer's garden harvest filled in the spaces; sliced fresh tomatoes, watermelon chunks, and sweet cantaloupe.

Katie carried out the last of her contributions to the feast – a big pan of fragrant apple cobbler made from the apples she grew herself. She managed to find a place to squeeze the pan in amongst a bevy of other desserts.

Katie's 16-year-old sister Sarah moved to stand next to her.

"Everything looks delicious. I hope Daniel Troyer gets to try my peanut butter pie."

Katie turned a stern eye on Sarah. "And why would that be?"

Katie couldn't help but notice the pink blossom in Sarah's cheeks and tried hard to hide her smile. She was very aware that her little sister had a crush on the young man who was two years older than Sarah.

Finally, Katie gave up her hardnosed act and reached out and touched her little sister's hand. Since their parents had been killed three years ago in a buggy accident Katie had taken responsibility for Sarah and their two brothers, 15-year-old Isaac and 9-year-old Jedidiah. Although she'd only been twenty-one years old when her parents were killed, Katie was already a widow herself, her husband having died from a brain aneurism just two months after they'd married. After his death she'd moved back home with her family and it was only natural that she took on the care of her siblings when her parents passed.

"Well, Sarah, if you get your wish I'm sure he'll find it delicious. You have a natural talent for baking. Who wouldn't love your pie? Now, let's get some of this food before it's all gone."

The crowd was famished and made quick work of devouring the multitude of edible offerings after Bishop Yoder finished his longwinded prayer. It wasn't long before groans of contentment echoed throughout the newly constructed space and more than one person rubbed their belly with satisfaction.

Katie was hustling back to the house to grab more apple cider just as Yon Hochstetler rose from the bench where he'd sat for the evening meal. She jerked to a stop just prior to crashing into the big man. Color seeped into her cheeks. She couldn't help it. Yon Hochstetler was a good looking man and quite a talented woodworker. He had a successful business making and selling custom-built furniture. Even though he was nearing thirty years old he had never married. He'd come to Serenity Falls a couple years ago, moving here from Lancaster, Pennsylvania to be near his brother Amos who had brought his family to Indiana several years earlier.

"Please excuse me, Katie." Yon's hand went to the brim of his hat. "I wasn't watching."

Katie cast her eyes downward, feeling awkward, as usual, when she was in the big man's presence.

"No, I shouldn't have been moving so fast. I just can't seem to go slow sometimes."

"Well, you must be on an important mission."

"Oh, very important. We're almost out of apple cider."

Yon threw his head back and laughed. "Well, we certainly can't run out of apple cider. Come on, I'll help you carry out more."

It was already growing dark on this evening in late September as she and Yon strolled across the yard towards the house. A brisk breeze kicked up and whipped Katie's burgundy dress against her legs. She raised a hand to hold her *kapp* on as a particularly mischievous gust threatened to blow it off her red-gold curls.

"I'm glad the wind was gentler this afternoon when I was crawling around on the rafters of the new barn," Yon commented. "It might have blown me away."

Katie giggled at the mental image of big, brawny Yon sailing across the sky, tumbling about in the wind currents.

"Oh, so the thought of me getting blown away is funny, is it?" Yon quirked his sable brown eyebrows at her. "I must say, Katie, that isn't very Christian of you."

Planting her feet and placing her hands on her hips Katie turned and scolded him. "And you are teasing me, Yon Hochstetler, which isn't very Christian of you, so I guess we're even."

A smile crept across his face, exposing strong white teeth. "*Jah*, I guess we are at that."

Katie watched curiously as Yon' smile disappeared and he suddenly froze, his concentration focused on the horizon.

"I see smoke. And now I see flames, too. There's another fire." Yon's voice sounded tense, worried. "It looks like it's over on Middle Creek Road."

Katie turned sharply to take in the sight of smoke roiling into the dusky sky. She drew in a sharp breath, her hand clenching at the bodice of her black apron.

"My house is on Middle Creek Road."

"No, it's too far west for your place." He didn't say anything else for a long minute. "But it sure looks like it could be mine."

CHAPTER 2 - FIRE STARTER

Everything seemed to happen in fast motion after that. Katie's feet flew to the phone box at the edge of the road, her fingers shaking as she dialed 911. Men scurried to their buggies and headed out in force towards the flickering flames while women quickly gathered up their children. She found her three siblings and sent them home with their great Aunt Esther and Uncle Joe.

"Come on, Katie." The voice of her best friend Ruth Voorhees broke into Katie's troubled thoughts as she watched her family roll away. "We're making coffee to take to those fighting the fire. Why don't you come help us?"

Katie nodded and moved towards the house but a worried frown stayed painted on her face. Another fire so soon after the one that burnt the Gruber's barn down was a shock. Then there was the added worry that there had been little rain over the summer and the countryside was a dried up tinderbox. The creeks had shriveled into small streams, the landscape parched and thirsty. The wind gusted vigorously, making dust devils whirl across the fields. Fire in these conditions was a major threat.

The women quickly brewed several vats of strong coffee and loaded it into their buggies. Katie shivered and pulled her black shawl closer around her shoulders before picking up the reigns and clicking to her horse Daisy. The big mare started off at a brisk clip, uncaring that full darkness had fallen in the past few minutes.

It wasn't hard to find the way. Even if she didn't live on the same road the billows of smoke and skyrocketing sparks would have led her right to the burning structure.

Katie's heart sank as she came upon the scene. Just as Yon feared, it was his property going up in flames. The large workshop where he crafted his furniture was quickly crumbling into a pile of steaming rubble. The volunteer fire department of Serenity Falls had arrived and pumped gallons of water onto the flaming building, the fire snapping and crackling in rebuke.

Katie found Yon sitting on the back steps of his house watching as his livelihood disintegrated before his eyes. The eerie light cast by the flames and the strobing beams from the fire trucks cast him in a pool of reds and oranges. Black streaks of soot creased across his face.

"Yon, I'm so sorry."

For a long moment Yon simply bowed his head before he spoke.

"It is so hard to comprehend. It's gone, all gone. My tools, my inventory, the merchandise for my orders. I think even my old cat Hezekiah was in there."

Katie didn't know what to say. She was no stranger to grief but she'd never grown comfortable with it. She found the words strangled in her throat, unable to express her feelings. Instead of speaking she simply placed a hand on Yon's broad shoulder, hoping he would feel her compassion for him even if she couldn't put it into words.

"But, I must not despair." Yon squared his shoulders and lifted his chin and looked calmly into her eyes. "I must trust in *Gott* to see me through this trouble. *Gott* is our refuge and strength, a very present help in trouble."

Katie recognized the verse from Psalm 46. It was one of her favorites, one she'd recited to herself many times after the death of her husband and her parents.

"Therefore we will not fear though the earth gives way, though the mountains be moved into the heart of the sea, though its waters roar and foam, though the mountains tremble at its swelling." She spoke the next verse softly, clinging to the comforting words and a small smile played across his lips as he rose to his feet.

"Here comes the fire chief. I'm sure he wants to talk to me." They both watched as Mitch Kendall, an Englisher who owned an auto dealership in Serenity Falls, walked in their direction. He was also chief of the town's volunteer fire department. A short, stocky man he strode towards them with a serious expression on his bulldog-like face.

"Yon, sorry about your place. Unfortunately, it looks like a total loss. It had a good head start when we got here."

"I understand, Mitch. I appreciate what you and your team have done."

Mitch hesitated, turning the brim of his yellow helmet in his hands.

"You see, here's the thing, Yon. This fire appears to have been set exactly like the fire at the Gruber's barn last week." He cleared his throat before continuing. "These fires were both arson. Oh, I'll have an inspector out to confirm it but it's obvious an accelerant was poured all around the building, just like at the Gruber's."

Katie heard the words but her mind was slow to accept them. Surely he didn't mean someone was going around setting these fires deliberately?

Yon, too, looked dazed. "I don't understand. Why would someone want to burn my property? Or the Gruber's barn? They even lost one of their best horses in that fire."

Mitch raised a hand and ran it through his stubbly salt and pepper hair, scratching his head.

"Well, that's what I don't get. Normally, the first suspects would be the property owners, after the insurance money and all. But most Amish folks don't believe in buying insurance. You wouldn't be an exception to that rule now, would ya?"

"No. Like the rest of my order, I do not have any insurance. We trust in *Gott* to take care of our needs."

Mitch grimaced and nodded. "I was afraid you'd say that. So that leaves us at square one. I'm going to have to involve the law, get some investigators on it."

Yon looked directly into Mitch's eyes when he spoke. "You know my people prefer to handle their own problems. We don't like to involve outsiders, not even the police."

"I know that, Yon, but this is not a case I can ignore. Arson is a serious crime and, just think, man, in these weather conditions it's even more dangerous. If we've got a fire bug on the loose, anything could happen. He could set the whole dang town on fire. Lives could be lost and that's not just an Amish problem; it's a threat to the entire community. We're bringing in the law. Now."

Yon didn't speak a word, just folded his hands in front of him and looked towards the scene of the now dying fire. Katie turned her gaze as well, taking in the pile of destruction then sweeping it across the gathered crowd. Was one of these people an arsonist? Someone she had known all her life?

She let her eyes rest on Eli Zook, the simple minded man child who at 25 still had the intelligence of an 8 year old. He stood staring, mesmerized, at the sputtering flames. She remembered seeing him stare that same hypnotized way into bonfires they had attended together over the years.

And there was Sam Miller, the teenager who had accidentally set fire to his family's barn when he was playing with matches and it got out of hand. Or Joseph Klingemann, the blacksmith who always seemed angry. Plus all those townspeople who might have some kind of grudge against the Amish.

So who was burning down Amish properties? Katie didn't know the answer. She just had a bad feeling this wasn't going to end good.

CHAPTER 3 - THE AGREEMENT

Katie stopped at Aunt Esther's and Uncle Joe's house on the way home from the fire and picked up her brothers and sister. She took a few moments to talk with her aunt and uncle then hustled the children towards their own home. It was much later than they usually went to bed and everyone would be tired in the morning. Jedidiah was practically asleep by the time she pulled the buggy into the barnyard.

It didn't take long for the household to quiet down for the night and Katie fell eagerly onto her own bed. It had been a long day and her body was exhausted. Unfortunately, her mind didn't feel the same way. Questions raced through her head, one chasing after another. Who had set the fires? Was it really a firebug, a serial arsonist initiating his trail of flames? Or could Mitch Kendall be mistaken? Maybe the fires really had been accidental and he was just jumping to conclusions. Katie prayed that was the answer.

Morning came far too soon for Katie. She'd slept little and when she did manage to doze off she dreamt of all-consuming flames devouring everything in their path. When the rooster crowed she groaned before dragging herself out of the bed. Time to start the day, ready or not.

"Jed, stop playing with your food and eat," Katie admonished her little brother. "Isaac, what are your plans this morning?"

Isaac reached for another piece of toast and spread it with spicy apple butter. "After I take Sarah to work I thought I'd get the last of the apples picked and keep an eye on the fruit stand. Jed can help me."

"Sounds good. Listen, I have an idea I have to run past the three of you."

Three hours later Katie had the dishes washed and a load of laundry drying on the line. She climbed into the buggy Isaac had hitched up for her and gave Daisy a cluck and they set off down the road. First she would go past Miller's Variety Store where Sarah worked and pick up some more material so she could make Jedidiah a new pair of pants. The boy was sprouting up so fast she could barely keep his ankles covered. Next, she had a mission to accomplish.

When she arrived at the store there were already a couple other buggies pulled in the lot alongside several automobiles. Englishers were fond of shopping here for a variety of Amish goods. She greeted neighbors who were also there to buy supplies (and share a little gossip). Naturally the talk centered around the recent fires. Word had already gotten around that both blazes had been deliberately set and speculation was high. No one had a clue who in their tiny community might be guilty of arson.

Katie was no closer to an answer when she plopped her package onto the buggy seat and turned the horse back towards Middle Creek Road. The sun was high in the sky by now and the air ripe with the rich fragrances of autumn. Rays of light shimmered between a canopy of jewel toned leaves, bathing the road with dancing shadows.

The light is pleasant, and it is gut for the eyes to see the sun. The verse from Ecclesiastes popped into her head as Daisy trotted along. It described this beautiful day perfectly. She whispered a little prayer to thank *Gott* for nature's splendor even when times were troubled.

Katie turned Daisy into Yon Hochstetler's driveway. Her gaze immediately went to the rubble left by the fire and her spirits dropped. What a waste. All Yon's hard work, his tools and his supplies gone; gone with the single action of a deranged mind.

And that's why she was here. She thought she had a solution to Yon's immediate problem.

Katie was just climbing down from the buggy when she heard Yon call a greeting. He strode towards her from the direction of the small shed at the rear of his property, his hand raised in greeting.

"*Gut* morning, Katie." Despite what Katie knew must have been a night even more sleepless than her own Yon looked cheerful and ready to take on the new challenges of the day.

"*Jah* and a beautiful morning it is." Katie ran a hand across her apron to smooth any wrinkles and walked towards Yon. She laughed as his fat old hound dog waddled towards her, his tail wagging in greeting. "And hello to you, too, Bandit." The dog had been named for the dark mask across his eyes.

The dog stayed close to where Yon and Katie stood talking in the yard. They made no move to go into the house. Katie had no desire to give gossiping tongues any reason to wag and planned to stay in plain sight while she visited with the handsome bachelor.

"Yon, I've been thinking. You know my father was also a woodworker and furniture maker. His workshop still stands, basically untouched. Isaac has shown little interest in learning the trade, he is more attracted to the orchards and the animals. There are all the tools you need and many supplies. You are welcome to its use until you can reconstruct your shop."

"Oh, Katie. I couldn't. That is too generous." Yon smiled sadly. "I do thank you sincerely, though."

"Now, Yon please don't say no. Actually, you would be doing me a favor. *Daett's* tools have barely been touched since his passing. They're just deteriorating out there. You could bring them back to life, make them productive again. It would be *gutt* to see them being used.

Yon didn't speak for several moments. A myriad of emotions flickered across his face. She saw a mixture of hope, uncertainty, and consideration in his eyes.

"Please, Yon. I've already discussed it with the family and we all agree it is the right thing to do."

Finally he gave his head a firm nod.

"Okay, we'll try it. But you must promise that if I become any trouble, if I am in the way at all, you will tell me and we will end this arrangement. And I will pay you rent for the use of the premises."

"That's not necessary. I just want to see my father's tools being used again and to help a neighbor in times of trouble. Besides, *Gott* said "Do not neglect to do good and to share what you have, for such sacrifices are pleasing to *Gott*.""

"Danka, Katie." Yon's grin spread wide across his face. "You are a *gut* friend."

Katie felt a spot in her heart begin to warm.

"Fine. We'll see you tomorrow then?

"Jah. Tomorrow morning first thing."

CHAPTER 4 - SUSPICIOUS EYES

Katie slept little better that night than she had the night before. Again she had dreams of burning fires but this time the dreams mingled with past losses. She dreamt her parents were consumed by fire even though she knew they died when their buggy was crushed by a drunk driver. There was no fire involved.

Later her night visions focused on her husband James. They had been married only two months when she watched him collapse and die at the breakfast table, a brain aneurysm taking him almost immediately. Now, though, her dreams pictured him seated at a table circled by flames that inched towards him. She tried to save him, tried with all her might, but she wasn't fast enough. She awoke with a start just before the flames began devouring him.

Despite the cool late September night air, Katie woke in a pool of sweat, her blankets twisted around her body. It was early, not even light yet, but she knew she wouldn't be able to sleep anymore. She dragged herself from bed and headed down stairs to make coffee.

Two hours after rising she'd already scrubbed the kitchen floor, gathered the eggs, and had breakfast on the stove as her siblings stumbled out of bed. A few moments late Katie heard the sound of buggy wheels crunching up the drive. She peered out the curtainless kitchen window and saw Yon pulling up in front of the barn.

Katie moved to open the back door and wave him inside.

"*Gut* morning, Yon. You are just in time for breakfast."

"No, no, I'm fine. I had a bowl of cereal before I left home."

"That's not enough for a big man like you. Come, sit, have some pancakes and sausage." Katie hustled around the kitchen setting plates for everyone. Yon looked slightly uncomfortable but sank into the indicated chair.

"*Danka*, Katie. But I do not want you to go to extra trouble for me."

"Don't be silly; there's plenty."

Her brothers and sister scrambled to the table and thirty minutes later Yon was grinning. "*Danka* again, Katie. That was delicious. A bachelor sometimes gets tired of eating his own bad cooking all alone."

"Well, that's what you get for staying a bachelor all these years," she replied tartly. "Now come, let me show you *Daett's* workshop."

Together they headed across the back yard towards her father's workshop that had stood so silent and still for so long. She opened the door into the square building and moved aside so Yon could pass her.

He took in the complete shop with a sweeping gaze. Shelves and pegboards held neatly lined up tools and a large tool bench took up a portion of the back wall. Everything was neat and tidy, just the way *Daett* had left it. Katie came out here every week and wiped the dust away, her heart aching with the loss of her parents. She'd tried to step in and be a good caretaker of her brothers and sister but knew she would never replace their *Maemm* and *Daett*.

"This is excellent." Yon looked about with a satisfied smile. "It looks like everything I need is here."

"I'm glad you can use it. It will be good to smell sawdust out here again." Katie nodded firmly then turned to head back to the house. It was time to deliver the baked goods and apple butter that she sold to a popular restaurant in Serenity Falls. The small town attracted a fair number of tourists who came to visit the many local arts and crafts stores and experience a bit of the Amish lifestyle. Katie's pies and other baked goods were in big demand.

Once again it was a sunny day, warm already for this late in September. Katie didn't even need to wear her shawl as she drove into town. Fifteen minutes after she'd headed out she pulled up behind Yoder's Café. Mary Yoder greeted her warmly and urged her to stop and enjoy a soft drink.

"So have you heard any news about the arsonist?"

Katie shook her head. "No, nothing new."

"My cousin Bishop Yoder says this is the work of a messenger of *Gott*, someone who is warning us about Hell fire." Mary leaned close, her voice a conspirator's whisper.

That didn't surprise Katie. Bishop Yoder was the head of her *Ordnung* and certainly had her respect but he was a gloomy character and his favorite sermon topics were fire and brimstone. She herself preferred to think as *Gott* as a more loving father and provider than a threat to be feared and trembled before.

Katie chose to take the diplomatic way out and simply nodded as she sipped at her cola and a family of travelers walked in the front door at that moment. Mary hurried off to take their order and Katie was spared having to respond.

A few minutes late Katie waved goodbye at Mary and headed out the back door. She was still a few feet from her buggy when a large form rumbled around the corner and she nearly smacked into a wall of flesh.

"Well, if it isn't the prettiest Amish woman in Indiana."

Hot pink scalded Katie's cheeks. She'd confronted Wade McFadden before. He owned the local tavern and was probably considered quite handsome in the eyes of many English women but something about him repulsed Katie and a shiver of fear ran down her spine. She didn't like the way he looked at her.

Though it was only midmorning Katie could smell beer on Wade's breath. He stood too close, his gaze too bold as it scraped across her body from her *kapp*, over her forest green dress and down to her toes. She'd heard rumors about him. Word was that he was a convicted felon who somehow came up with the wherewithal to buy the tavern in Serenity Falls. She was also aware that McFadden had no respect for the Amish.

Katie drew her dignity around her like a cape. She wasn't about to let this oversized man intimidate her.

"*Gut* morning, Mr. McFadden."

"*Gut* morning to you, too, pretty lady." McFadden over exaggerated the *g* in *gut*, a sneer tugging at his lips. Katie couldn't help it. She felt his disdain for her people and fought to control her temper. She should not let herself be provoked by his disrespectful attitude.

"So, I hear you Amish folks are having a hot time lately." He chuckled at his own joke. "Getting things fired up around here."

The gleeful look in McFadden's eyes sent a cold chill slithering down her spine. He seemed much too happy about the situation.

Katie stood stock still and stared at him. Was she looking into the eyes of the arsonist?

CHAPTER 5 - ANOTHER DEAD END

Katie hurriedly made her excuses and climbed into her buggy, eager to get away from Wade McFadden. The Englisher made her uncomfortable. She breathed a sigh of relief when she was able to guide Daisy down the alley and onto the street, leaving the hungry eyes of McFadden behind her.

She started to heads towards home then had an idea. Instead of going back to the house she turned the horse towards the library. She wanted some answers and she might be able to find them on the internet.

Although Bishop Yoder didn't like modern technology her *Ordnung* had decided it was okay to use if for business purposes, their members just weren't allowed to have it in their homes. Katie knew this wasn't exactly business but in a way it was. She felt as if it were all the local Amish people's business to find this firebug and put an end to his evil ways before more of them lost their property…or maybe even their lives.

Katie had used a computer several times before when she helped out at the yarn and quilt store where she sold many of her handcrafted goods online. It didn't take her long to find what she was looking for. Unfortunately, what she discovered was all bad news.

Not only was Wade McFadden a felon, he'd been convicted of arson. He'd been found guilty of setting fire to his own home in order to collect the insurance money and spent a year in prison. He'd lived in Indianapolis then and the incident happened over a decade ago. Katie wasn't sure how he'd managed to come to own the bar in Serenity Falls but she did know he held the Amish in contempt. He'd cornered her once before when she was leaving Yoder's Café and made his opinion of them clear. Actually called them ignorant Neanderthals.

So now she had this information. What should she do with it?

Isaac met her in the drive and led Daisy off to the barn. Jed came running up, a new rip in the knee of his pants, a happy smile creasing his freckled face.

"Oh, Jed, another pair of pants I need to mend. What am I going to do with you, you little imp?"

"Maybe you should teach him to mend them himself." Yon spoke as he strode across the yard. "I know as a bachelor I've had to wield a needle and thread now and then."

"That's a fine idea, Yon. Okay, Jed, after supper tonight I'll give you a sewing lesson. Now, go see if Isaac needs any help with Daisy."

"Okay." Jed ran full speed ahead across the yarn, his feet churning up clouds of dust on the dry path.

"I'd like to talk to you, Yon, if you have a minute."

"Sure, sure. What can I do for you?"

"Let's set on the porch in the shade while we talk."

Once they'd settled Katie began telling him about her encounter with Wade McFadden and filled him in on what she'd learned.

"He's set fires before, Yon."

Yon ran a hand across his chin. "True, but there is nothing to indicate he's involved in these fires."

"He really dislikes Amish. He thinks our people are ignorant and inflexible." Katie couldn't disregard the uneasy feeling she had about the barkeeper. "Would he do this just to harass us?"

"If he would, I think that proves who is really the ignorant one." Yon scowled, his dark eyebrows drawing together, before he continued speaking.

"Sheriff Weeks came to see me yesterday afternoon. He says they're investigating but still don't have a suspect. I wonder if he knows about McFadden's record?"

"Do you think we should tell him?"

"We Amish take care of our own, but in this case I think taking care of us best involve the law. *Jah*. I'll go by his office on my way home. He may already know but I want to make sure he does." Yon rose to his feet. "Now I'll take myself back to your *Daett's* fine shop and get back to work."

Katie continued to set for a few more minutes, thoughts racing through her mind. Yon was right. There was no proof that McFadden had anything to do with setting these fires. Maybe she was the one jumping to conclusions. Or perhaps it was even wishful thinking. She didn't want to believe someone from her *Ordnung* could be responsible.

Whoever it was she felt sorry for them. Only a sick mind could enjoy destroying other people's property and putting lives at risk. This was a person crying out for help. She prayed to *Gott* they would find him in time to save both him and those whose lives he endangered.

CHAPTER 6 - SEPTEMBER SUNDAY

The next few days were uneventful. The long dry spell continued and the days seemed to fall into a pattern. Yon showed up early, often in a wagon loaded with supplies. He often had breakfast with Katie and the children before heading to the workshop.

Katie was surprised to find that both her brothers began spending much of the day with Yon, helping him sand and finish and paint. The amount of interest they had shown in Yon's work amazed her. After she thought about it, though, she realized the boys probably would have taken more of an interest in woodworking earlier if their father hadn't died at such a young age. Now they had a man to mentor them and teach them how to use the tools and create handcrafted pieces.

Yon found time to pull her aside and tell her that he had spoken to Sheriff Weeks about Wade McFadden. It turned out that not only did the police already now about McFadden's record but had already talked to him and eliminated him as a suspect. He had an ironclad alibi for the nights the fires had been set. He'd been tending bar and had a dozen customers as witnesses to his presence both days.

No more fires occurred that week and some of the tension began to ease out of Katie's body. Maybe the arsonist was finished. He might be scared of being caught and decided to give up his dangerous fire starting. Maybe the culprit had been just someone passing through the area and was long gone now. Katie decided she was going to take an optimistic attitude and not look for trouble.

It was her turn to host church that Sunday so she, Sarah, and the boys put in hours of preparation. She and Sarah cleaned the house from top to bottom making sure every window sparkled and every floor gleamed. They spent hours in the kitchen baking, making noodles, and cooking up a large batch of applesauce.

The boys prepared the barn, sweeping it until there wasn't a straw out of place. The lawn was mowed and everything was as neat as it could possibly be made. Pride was a sin so Katie chose to call the emotion she felt as she gazed over the immaculate property contentment. Many people, especially Aunt Esther and Uncle Joe, did not think Katie would be able to provide for her siblings after her parents died. Even though she was a widow they felt she would be too young and immature to guide the younger Bontragers on the proper path, but she had proved them wrong.

It hadn't been easy. Not only did she have to take on the duties of both parents she had to figure out how to make ends meet financially. Fortunately she had a talent both in the kitchen and with a needle. Her quilts demanded a hefty price from English buyers willing to pay for craftsmanship. She also ran a road side fruit stand and sold produce from her garden and orchards, fresh eggs, honey, and pumpkins in the fall.

She didn't mind the hard work. It kept her busy and kept her mind off her losses. She had barely begun to know her husband when he was taken from her and soon after she lost both her parents at once. She thought perhaps if it wasn't for the daily demands that kept her focused she might have lost her mind.

And then there were the suitors to deal with. An assortment of men had come calling on her; they were certain she would be desperate enough she would accept them. There had been Jacob Saul, the widowed father of 10 children. Then Abraham Miller had come around. She couldn't help it; something about the scarecrow of a man made her feel creepy.

Even Bishop Yoder had asked to court her. The fact that he was old enough to be Katie's grandfather didn't seem to bother him and when she turned him down he became angry and began ranting and preaching at her. It hadn't been easy but she had stood her ground and he'd finally given up his courtship.

Now she gazed around the Bontrager farm and a sense of satisfaction filled her. *Gott* was good. He had blessed them with fruitful land and healthy bodies to work it.

A moment later buggies began to roll up the drive and greetings rang through the air. Children escaped from the carriages and ran across the yard, squealing and laughing as they greeted each other. Men unloaded benches from the wagons and began carrying them into the barn.

The church service lasted all morning. By the time it was over everyone was ready to eat. Mountains of food were served and all the women pitched in offerings. Afterwards the men played horseshoes and the children played baseball. Once the cleanup was complete the women were content to set and watch the others and share in conversation. Who had a baby, who was courting who, cooking, and child care were all favorite topics.

By late afternoon most of the adults packed up their children and went home. All that were left were the young people who would be staying for the singing that evening. Singings were traditional for Amish teens nearing the age of courtship and usually took place on church Sundays. It was a time when they could talk and get to know each other. Katie noticed that Sarah took a seat across from Daniel Troyer but was pretending to ignore him. Katie couldn't hide a smile as she watched. Oh, how she remembered those days when she was that young and fresh faced and falling head over heels for James. Before she had begun a personal relationship with grief.

Hosting the singing was part of the duties of the family who hosted church, so it was up to Katie to chaperone the group. When Yon approached her and volunteered to stick around she smiled gratefully. Having another adult here would ease her burden of responsibility.

Yon and Katie retreated to the porch where they could see into the open barn doors. Soon the sounds of lively music filled the air and Katie couldn't help but hum along.

It was a beautiful evening, warm and crystal clear. Stars poked their shiny heads out, twinkling and winking at those below. A slight breeze tickled through the trees and a huge orange harvest moon crept over the horizon.

Yon stretched his legs and grinned. "I feel like we should be taking part in the singing."

"Don't you think we're a little old for that?"

"*Jah*, probably. But I must confess being with you makes me feel young."

Katie shot him a sideways glance then quickly looked away. She had refused to think about it right up to this moment but she had to admit she felt herself drawn to Yon. No doubt he was a handsome man but it was more than that. It was how kind he was to her siblings, the patient way he showed the boys how to hold a tool or plane a surface. It was something about the way he laughed often and heartily, his joy for life. The look on his face when he patted his old dog Bandit, a kindness in his soul that seemed to shine from his eyes.

Katie couldn't find the words to answer Yon. For some reason it seemed she was tongue tied and the look she felt him giving her made her words catch in her throat.

But suddenly her attention was distracted from the man sitting beside her. Her gaze was drawn to the southern sky. No, please, *Gott*, don't let that be smoke she was seeing.

CHAPTER 7 - BEWARE THE FIRES OF HELL

"Yon." She only managed to say his name then pointed to the south. He turned his gaze to follow her finger and she heard his breath catch in his chest.

"It's happening again, Katie. Fire." Yon stood up and tensed as he gazed at the horizon, puffs of smoke now beginning to fill the sky. "Quick, run to the phone box and call the fire department."

It seemed like de ja vu after that. Once again Katie found her feet flying down the drive to the phone box at the end of the lane. Once again Yon was in his buggy racing past her towards the site were flames licked the sky.

Katie made quick work of dispersing the young people towards their own homes. She, too, was anxious to head out and find where the fire was. From the location of the flames, she had an awful feeling that Miller's Variety Store was engulfed.

Katie ordered the children to go inside then climbed in the buggy and headed Daisy in the direction of the fire. As she had feared, the Amish store was going up in flames.

Even more frightening than the sight of the burning store surrounded by the strobing lights of the fire trucks was the ambulance pulled up in the lot. Its back doors were just being slammed shut and the driver hustled around to climb inside. She watched silently, her fist pressed to her lips as the ambulance sped away towards town.

This time someone had been hurt, maybe even killed. Anxiously she looked about for someone to tell her who was in that ambulance.

She spotted Yon heading her way and hurried to meet him.

"Yon, who was in the ambulance? Are they…alive?" Her voice broke when she blurted out her question.

"It was Ruth Miller and yes she is alive but just barely." Yon's eyes were worried, his expression grave. "She suffered smoke inhalation. She wasn't breathing when they first found her but they got her resuscitated. She's still in danger."

Katie closed her eyes and sent a heartfelt prayer heavenward. Ruth had seven children that needed her.

"Does anyone know why she was alone in the store on Sunday night?"

"Apparently she had come to finish up a big order that was due to be picked up in the morning. Baked goods, I guess. Thank *Gott* they just live up the road and husband Aaron saw the flames. He pulled her out just in time."

Just then a portion of the roof collapsed, crashing down and sending sparks high into the sky. The deafening noise sent Katie stumbling back with surprise. Her foot rolled on the loose gravel and she felt herself falling, helpless to stop herself from hitting the ground.

Yon instinctively reached out and grabbed Katie's arms, halting her backwards freefall. He jerked her forward and she almost went too far the other direction, threatening to slam into his chest. For a moment she just stood perfectly still, far too aware of his nearness.

Finally she found her voice.

"*Danka*, Yon. That could have been quite embarrassing. Now, I need to go talk to some of the other women. We'll want to make arrangements to get some meals to the Miller family while Ruth is in the hospital." She pulled free from the heat of his hands and headed across the lot but she only traveled a few feet before a loud voice froze her in position.

Bishop Yoder stood at the front of the gathered crowd, his hands raised, his gruff voice calling for attention. The dying flames cast eerie lights and shadows over his tall, lanky frame, his eyes appearing to be set in dark holes. His long scraggly beard ended in a point well below his chin and for a moment Katie thought he looked more like a devil than a servant of *Gott*.

"Hear me now people! This is a warning from *Gott*. I've cautioned you before. We must stop our sinful ways. Stop working on the Sabbath, bringing worldly values into our lives. Stop allowing our young people so much freedom during *rumpsringe*." The bishop may have been getting older but his voice was still strong and it rose in volume as he continued his rant. "These fires will not stop until we turn our backs on worldly ways. He told us in Isaiah 33:14 "Sinners in Zion are terrified; Trembling has seized the godless. Who among us can live with the consuming fire? Who among us can live with continual burning?"

Bishop Yoder raised a hand and pointed a bony finger at Noah Gruber. "You there, Brother Gruber. You suffered the loss of your barn and your best horse because you sinned. You use many power tools for your construction business. And you, Aaron Miller, mingling with Englishers constantly, using computers and electricity to run your business. Yon Hochstetler, you angered *Gott* by selling your goods on the internet. That is why you've all felt the heat of the flames. May *Gott* forgive you."

He paused for a long moment, all eyes on his angry face. "Who will feel the heat next? Will it be you, Katie Bontrager? You who thinks you're too good for any man who is willing to take on you and your siblings?" His long skinny finger pointed directly at Katie, his eyes burrowing into her with accusation. "Or maybe you, Mary Yoder, running a restaurant that caters to outsiders. Heed my warning, people, before it's too late and the fires of Hell consume us all."

With that he strode angrily across the yard and climbed into his buggy. The crowd was left in stunned silence as he turned his horse towards home.

CHAPTER 8 - DANGEROUS DISCOVERY

The next morning Katie still felt scorched by the bishop's heated words. As she stirred up a batch of biscuits for breakfast she thought about what he said. Was there any truth to his words? Was *Gott* punishing them for sinful ways?

She had a hard time conceding to that. Those in her *Ordnung* limited their use of technology to the minimum, using it only enough to insure their financial survival. No matter how hard they clung to the Plain life, they had to support themselves in honorable ways. And as far as *rumpsringe* went that is what the running around time was meant for. It gave their young people an opportunity to explore other ways, to determine if they were willing to commit to the Amish way of life forever. Yes, they had more options to discover now, but that was just the way it was today.

The words he hurled at her specifically kept replaying through her mind. He'd accused of her thinking herself too good, too prideful, to accept any of the men as her husband after James died. It wasn't that at all. She didn't think she was better than anyone else. But she had been married. She knew the intimacy involved and she simply had not met a man she was willing to share those tender moments with.

A sudden vision of Yon floated through her mind. She finished placing the biscuits on the baking pan and turned to shove them in the oven. At least the heat from the stove would give her an excuse for her reddened cheeks if Sarah happened to turn around from where she was setting places at the table.

Yon didn't appear for breakfast that morning. In fact he didn't show up until after lunch. Katie was in the back yard hanging freshly washed laundry when he finally pulled his buggy into the long drive.

After greeting her Yon said, "I stopped to talk to the Sheriff before I came out."

"Any news?"

"Just that this fire was set just like the others. The same accelerant was used in all three fires. Oddly enough it's charcoal lighter fluid."

"Well, that's easily obtainable. Anyone can buy it at almost any store. So it doesn't narrow down the suspect list much, does it?" Katie sighed and shook her head. "Have you heard how Ruth is doing?"

"She's holding her own."

Katie whispered a prayer of thanksgiving. No one should lose their life in a fire deliberately set by an arsonist.

Later that afternoon Katie made a decision to ride into the farm supply store in Serenity Falls. She needed more canning jars to finish up the last of the tomatoes. She planned on making ketchup and salsa and had already used her supplies.

The day was hot and sunny, though a restless breeze tossed the grasses covering the fencerows she passed as she headed into town. The humidity was high, the air thick and hard to breathe. Maybe that was a good sign. Maybe rain was finally on the way.

Katie hurried through her errands and rolled her shopping cart out to the parking lot where Daisy patiently waited. She noticed another buggy parked directly next to hers and recognized Bishop Yoder as he loaded cartons into his closed carriage.

She nodded a greeting but only received an angry glare in return. Fine. She really didn't want to talk to him either. She made quick work of loading her own purchases into her buggy and quickly turned her horse towards home.

The house felt strangely empty when she arrived home. Yon had already quit for the day and her brothers and sister had headed over to the Miller farm to help them with their evening chores. With their mother in the hospital and their father staying by their side the young Millers could use all the help they could get. Sarah was going to cook their supper and the boys would take care of the livestock.

It felt funny to sit at the table by herself and eat a hamburger she had fried. She ate slowly, lost in her thoughts. Something was bothering her but she couldn't put her finger on just what it was.

She wiped down the table and washed up the few dishes she had dirtied before going to the porch to sit and meditate for a few minutes. She loved to watch the sun go down, painting the horizon with a palette of colors, listening to the sounds of nature's night life tuning up for their evening performance.

Tonight, though, a few scattered dark clouds blocked out much of the sunset view. Heat lightning speared the sky and the breeze murmured restlessly through the trees.

Katie finally began to relax a bit. She stopped trying to figure out what had been bothering her since her trip into town and instead tried to focus on all the blessings in her life.

And then it hit her like a sledge hammer whacking her in the head. She knew what had been disturbing her all evening. The cardboard box Bishop Yoder was loading into his buggy was labeled charcoal lighter fluid.

She knew who was setting the fires.

Katie rushed into the house and grabbed her shawl. She had to get word to Yon. She had to tell him what she'd discovered. Then they needed to get to the sheriff.

Katie drew her shawl around her shoulders, not only to shut out the brisk wind that had begun to blow but to warm the chill that had settled in her blood. Reaching the barn she tugged the door open and headed directly to Daisy's stall.

"So *Gott* has answered my prayers and sent you to me."

Katie froze still as a statue as the raspy voice of Bishop Yoder swept over her. He was here, the arsonist, alone with her. She turned slowly around until she could see him in the dim light of the barn. He stood there like a towering demon, his left hand clutching a bottle of charcoal lighter, a long lighter in his right.

"I prayed you would come, Katie. I asked *Gott* to send you as a sign that He knows that I am doing His work. And here you are. Now all will see what happens to a sinful person. They burn in the fires of Hell."

Katie noted the maniacal look in his eyes, the steady flicking of his thumb against the wheel of the lighter, the flame flicking on, then off, on, then off. She knew at that moment that she was gazing into the eyes of insanity.

She took a cautious step backwards. She didn't know how she was going to get away from him but she knew if she didn't she was going to die.

"You know it was wrong to turn down my offer of courtship, Katie. You know any woman should be honored to be the wife of the bishop." He took a step closer to her and she took another step back only to find her spine pressed against the rough wooden boards of the stall. "But no, not you. You are full of pride. You are a sinner."

She had to buy time. She had to stall him. Maybe the kids would come home or Aunt Esther or Uncle Joe would stop buy.

But who was she kidding. The kids wouldn't be home for another hour or two and her aunt and uncle were probably already in bed. She was all alone with a madman.

No, wait. She wasn't alone. She was never alone. *Gott* was always with her. A verse from Isaiah shouted in her ear. "The Lord is my helper; I will not be afraid. What can mere mortals do to me?"

And despite his many years of leadership, despite his years of service to *Gott*, Bishop Yoder was still a mere mortal. A mortal who had been overcome by sickness, by hate and poison in his system. She could, she must, escape from his malicious intent.

A quick surge of courage spouted through her and she charged forward. Her move was so unexpected that she managed to get past the crazy man and almost reached the door.

Almost.

She was only steps away from the portal to safety when his hand snatched onto her cape and hauled her backwards. The bishop drew her to him, his breath harsh and rasping. In another moment a pain exploded through Katie's head and her knees crumbled beneath her.

She didn't know if he'd hit her with his fist or some other weapon. She only knew that blackness threatened to engulf her and nausea rose in her throat from the blinding pain that blasted through her head. A trickle of dampness ran down her cheek and she knew she was bleeding.

Katie tried to fight him but her muscles were like overcooked spaghetti, limp and lifeless, weakened by the pain. A part of her mind was aware that he had a rope, that he was binding her to a post. She tried to focus as she watched in horror as he squirted the charcoal fluid around the barn, sending streams of it up the walls and pouring across bales of hay.

"Burn in the fires of Hell, Katie Bontrager."

With one last cackle of laughter Esau Yoder flicked the lighter on and watched the flickering light. Slowly, precisely, he leaned forward and held the flame to a straw bale and watched it ignite. Then, without another sound, he pushed out the barn door and disappeared from sight.

CHAPTER 9 - HOME FIRES BURNING

The fire started slowly. Just a few flames licking at the wooden walls, tiny blazes sprouting on a couple of hay bales. Katie blinked as she stared at the fiery tongues, trying to clear her blurry vision. She didn't need to be able to see clearly, though, to know that if she didn't do something fast she would die in this barn right along with Daisy and the other animals housed here.

Katie twisted and turned her hands in a frantic attempt to escape her bindings but her efforts only seemed to make them pull tighter. She doubled her efforts, tugging and jerking her wrists so desperately that she felt the rope bite into her flesh, chewing the skin raw.

She couldn't give up, wouldn't give up. Her thoughts flew to her brothers and sister. Dear *Gott*, they had already lost their parents. Surely he would not let them lose her, too. A vision of each of their faces passed through her mind.

There was Sarah, so sweet and kind. She would make Daniel Troyer a *gut* wife and mother to his children.

Next came Isaac. Such a hard worker, such a conscientious young man.

And then there was Jedidiah, the freckle faced imp who was always laughing. He had such a zest for life, a boundless curiosity which often led him into mischief.

A harsh cry broke from her throat as a picture of Yon flashed through her consciousness. He, too, had become a part of her family. Her heart couldn't lie. Yon was the only man that had affected her emotions since James, the only man she wanted in her life.

But if she didn't do something their future was about to go up in flames.

Smoke began to swirl through the air, making Katie cough and her eyes burn. The flames were growing now, streaking wickedly up the walls, sparks flying through the air.

"The Lord is my Shepherd, I shall not want." Katie's throat felt raw as she began to recite the 23 Psalm. The words came faster as she watched a trail of flames lick its way closer to her. "Yea, though I walk the valley of the shadow of death, I shall fear no evil."

The sudden thunderclap overhead sounded like the doors of Hell banging open. Katie refused to let the terror sway her faith. The Lord's will would be done. She only prayed that it was His will that somehow she would be saved from a fiery death.

Now the smoke was so thick Katie could barely see, the dense cloud filling her throat, shutting off her oxygen. A cascade of sparks rained down upon her face, burning and blistering. She could actually hear her *kapp* start to sizzle.

"Dear *Gott*, help me." She murmured the words as unconsciousness threatened to take her.

SHE THOUGHT she was dreaming when she felt strong hands lifting her, carrying her out of the burning barn and into the rain that had just begun to fall. Her head fell limply over Yon's supporting arm, her parched lungs struggling to draw in the damp air.

She heard Yon's prayers as though they came from a distance, heard him beg *Gott* to save her, to let her live. The sound of his voice urged her to breathe, to come back to him.

She struggled through the clouds of darkness that smothered her, finally managing to draw in one deep, shuddering breath. Her eyes blinked once, twice, then managed to focus on Yon's worried face. Somewhere she found the energy to draw herself up enough to wrap an arm around his neck.

"Bishop Yoder." Her voice was barely audible, rough and raspy from the smoke she'd swallowed.

"Hush, now. Don't try to talk. It's okay." He strode towards the porch with him still clutched in his arms. "I was with him when the farm store called him. He'd asked them to call him if anyone purchased a larger than usual amount of charcoal fluid. We found him a mile away, running down the road, laughing hysterically and still holding the bottle of lighter fluid. Sheriff Weeks is taking him to the hospital."

Katie let her throbbing head fall against Yon's shoulder. It was over. The nightmare was over.

"The fire department and ambulance are on their way," Yon informed her as he set her gently eased her down on a padded bench on the porch and sat beside her.

Katie turned her gaze to where her barn still stood, scorched and smoldering, but still intact. The rain pounded down, dousing the few flames that still fought to survive.

In the distance Katie heard the wail of approaching sirens but she knew it was too late for help from the fire department. *Gott* had already put out the blaze and sent an angel to save her.

At that moment a blaze of love ignited in Katie's heart. Gott had sent her a new beginning, a fresh start. Once her heart had been scorched, all her hopes and dreams for the future turned to ashes when James had been taken from her. She had planned to live out her life a widow, a caretaker for her siblings.

But now, now a new fire burned and new hope flamed to life.

"Katie, I believe *Gott* saved you for a reason." Yon softly spoke into her ear. "I believe he wants you to build fires. Home fires. Home fires to warm our heats, to feed our souls. What do you say? Should we keep the home fires burning?

She looked deep into his eyes before answering him with one word.

"Eternally."

Amish Investigation

THE PLEA BARGAIN

CHAPTER 1

"Charity, where have you been? I was worried about you," exclaimed Rebecca as Charity made her way through the perfect rows of potatoes.

Rebecca's tone changed from one of concern to annoyance when Charity waved her hand, dismissing her question. "You know how busy we are at harvest time; I can't believe you're late."

Rebecca straightened up. She put one hand on her lower back as she did. Her back gave an audible crack. Pulling the potatoes was hard work, made even harder when you had to do the work of two people.

"I'm sorry," Charity finally said. She bent to pull a potato, hoping it would hide her face from Rebecca. It didn't. She should have known Rebecca would notice. She was her best friend after all.

"Have you been crying? What's happened?" Rebecca crouched back down into the field and carried on pulling the potatoes. She regretted her annoyance now she saw her friend was upset.

"It's best you don't know. I don't want to drag you into this. If anyone asks, I was here when you got here. Ok?"

"No way," Rebecca said shaking her head firmly. "I'm not going to lie for you if I don't even know what's happened."

"You're my best friend," Charity said quietly.

"Exactly. You can trust me with the truth."

Charity sighed. She had known deep down that Rebecca would get it out of her. She always did when something was bothering her. She hadn't expected it to happen this quickly, but she did need to talk to someone about what she had heard, and she knew she could trust Rebecca.

"Swear to me you won't tell a soul," Charity said.

"I swear," Rebecca said. She sounded wary, but Charity trusted her. They had been best friends for as long as she could remember, and now they were closer than ever.

"I went to the trial," Charity said.

Rebecca gasped. "What? Why? What would have happened if your mother had found out you were missing?"

"She wouldn't," Charity said, ignoring the other question for now and concentrating on the one she knew she could answer. "I told her last night we had a really early start today and I would be gone before she got up. That's why I need you to say I was here when you got here."

"I don't understand why you would go there. Haven't you been through enough?"

"I had to. I had to hear it for myself."

"What happened?"

"Aaron got fifteen years," Charity said, her eyes filling with tears once more.

"I'm sorry Charity. It's not enough. Not anywhere near enough, but we have to trust in God. Aaron will face his true judgement when he faces God, not in a court room."

"You don't understand," Charity whispered.

"You're right. I can't even begin to imagine what it's like to lose your father. And then to find out that the animal who murdered him got off lightly. It must be like your whole world is crashing down around you."

Charity shook her head. "It's not that."

"Then what is it?"

Charity, who had been concentrating on the potato in front of her like all the answers to every question in the universe where on it looked up. She looked Rebecca square in the eye.

"I don't believe Aaron murdered my father. He's doing fifteen years of jail time for a crime he didn't commit."

"Are you crazy?" Rebecca blurted out. She lowered her voice. "I'm sorry, I didn't mean that to sound that way. But come on Charity. Why would you think he hadn't done it? The police believed he'd done it, and now the court has confirmed it. Even his own parents believe he did it."

"But I don't. What if they're wrong? You hear all the time of the police arresting people and then they get released because there was no evidence or whatever."

"True," Rebecca responded, "but how often do you hear of the person being found guilty when they're innocent?"

"Not very often," Charity conceded, "but it's possible."

"I suppose it is possible. But what I think is more possible is that you aren't seeing what's there. I get it. You liked

Aaron. A lot. Of course you don't want to think he did this. But he killed your father Charity. You can't lose sight of that."

Charity felt herself getting annoyed but she fought to keep her tone even, her words reasonable. "Do you think I don't know that? I loved my father Rebecca, and I want whoever killed him brought to justice, of course I do. But it wasn't Aaron. I'm sure of it."

"So how did the police and the court get it wrong?"

"The court didn't get a chance to hear any of it. Aaron pleaded guilty and there was no trial. As for the police, I have no idea how they could get it so wrong."

"There's your answer Charity. He pleaded guilty. What more proof could you possibly need?"

"I spoke to his lawyer after the sentencing. He told me that's how the law works. He could have insisted on a full trial and attempted to prove his innocence, but his lawyer said that often a jury will make an example out of an Amish person, you know, try to prove that we're not as pure as people believe. I don't know why.

"If this had gone to trial, he could have been facing the death penalty, or life without parole. Can you imagine that? He took what they call a plea bargain. He said he was guilty in exchange for a lighter sentence, so at least there's a hope of him getting out alive one day."

"I don't know," Rebecca said. "Surely if his lawyer believed he was innocent he would have pushed for a trial?"

Charity shrugged. "I don't know. Maybe he did push for a trial. Or maybe it's a case of there not being enough money in it for him so he wanted it over with quickly."

"And what about the police?"

"I don't know. Maybe they wanted the case closing quickly, so they pinned it on the nearest person."

"You sound like you're clutching at straws Charity," Rebecca said. Charity hated the pity she heard in her voice. She was humouring her and she knew it.

"Maybe," Charity said thoughtfully, "there's a lot I don't know, but I intend to find out. I'm not walking away from this Rebecca. For two reasons. Firstly, you're right. I do like Aaron, more than like him, I love him, and I'm not giving up on him until I know the truth. You didn't see his face in that court room. He looked so strained, so stressed. I've never seen him like that before. And secondly, I want whoever really did this caught. They deserve to be punished for killing my father."

"How do you plan on proving that Aaron is innocent, assuming he is?"

"I don't know yet, but I will think of something. I have to."

"You're going to have to sneak out a lot, and lie a lot to your mother. You realise that right?"

"Yes, I do. It's not something I like, but it is something I will have to do and suffer the consequences. I've thought about this a lot Rebecca, and having lying on my conscience won't be easy, but it will a whole lot easier than watching an innocent man serve a jail sentence I could have maybe prevented."

Rebecca paused for a second, stopping working to pick a piece of soil from under her finger nail. She didn't think Aaron was innocent. The police don't make mistakes like that. But she believed Charity thought he was, and she knew she wouldn't rest until she had proved it.

Maybe it would be for the best if Charity looked into it. At least then she would know the truth. That Aaron was guilty. It might give her some closure and allow her to move on.

"I don't like this, not one bit, but I know you'll do it anyway. I can't help you with this Charity, I don't want to become involved, but I will cover for you. If anyone asks, you were here before me this morning, and if you need to sneak off again, you can use me as cover."

"Thank you," Charity said. She smiled as her eyes filled with tears again. She reached out and hugged Rebecca.

Rebecca hugged her back. "We had better get on with this," she said indicating the field with a nod of her head. "These potatoes aren't going to harvest themselves."

CHAPTER 2

"Yoder, pick it up. This isn't a sewing club," shouted CO Benson.

The other men laughed and heckled him.

Aaron wondered if requesting to join the prison industries crew had been a mistake, but he had known he would go mad if he had nothing physical to do. He was used to hard work, and really, this was nothing compared to the work he was used to doing. If it wasn't for the COs and the other inmates constantly goading him, it could even be described as quite pleasant.

They were currently digging up a section of the prison yard to allow the maintenance crew access to the gas line. The sun was warm enough to raise a sweat and the fresh air was a welcome relief. Aaron had only been in here for four days and already he was regretting the decision to take the plea bargain.

His lawyer had thought it would be best, and stupidly, Aaron had trusted him. And now this was his life for the next fifteen years. He wasn't even sure if he could appeal. Was it possible to appeal a decision based on your own plea?

As he dug down again, he felt his spade connect with something harder than soil, and he heard the metallic clang of the gas line.

"Got it boss," he called to Benson.

The CO came over and peered into the trench they had dug.

"Go easy," he instructed. "We don't want the pipe cracking, just clear the rest of the dirt off the top and then go and wait over there until the maintenance crew are done. Once they're done, you all need to fill this back in."

The men muttered responses, and finished clearing the dirt. The six of them made their way to the grassy area they had been instructed to wait in. They sat down.

Aaron sat slightly away from the rest of them. He knew he should try to make friends, but it was something he struggled with. He had never really mixed with non-Amish men before, and they had very little common ground.

"Hey Yoder, what's up?" asked Jones, his cell mate, as he came to sit beside him on the grass.

"Hey," Aaron greeted him.

"How long you got?" Jones asked.

"Fifteen years," Aaron answered. "You?"

"Three years. I've got ten months left. Aggravated robbery."

"Murder," Aaron said. It still sounded so alien and wrong when he said it. "But it wasn't me. I took a plea bargain because that's what my lawyer recommended, but I didn't kill anyone."

"Sure you didn't," Jones said. "And I was just airing off my gun and I believed the store owner was donating to the cause."

Despite himself, Aaron laughed.

"We're all innocent in here mate," Jones said laughing with him.

Maybe it wouldn't be so bad after all Aaron thought. Jones seemed ok and as cell mates went he had learned quickly that it could be a whole lot worse.

A loud siren startled Aaron out of his thoughts. Jones jumped to his feet.

"What's happening?" Aaron asked as he too stood up and followed Jones.

"Lock down," Jones said. "Back to our cells."

"Lock down?"

"Twenty-four hour lock up. Our cells are going to get shaken down. You got any contraband?"

Aaron shook his head.

"Good," Jones smiled. "You can help me get rid of mine."

* * *

AARON WASN'T sure exactly what was happening, but their cell had been searched. They had reached it just in time for Jones to flush his stash as he had put it. Aaron wasn't sure he liked the idea of sharing a cell with a drug addict, but Jones had assured him they were just pain killers. He claimed the state wouldn't fund them because they didn't believe he had a back injury.

Aaron couldn't exactly blame them. He had watched Jones wield a spade, and he would have bet his last dollar there was nothing wrong with his back if he had been a gambling man. He decided the safest course of action was to agree with Jones.

It seemed to work. Jones was more upset about having to replace the pills than he was about Aaron seeming sceptical about his back. That suited Aaron down to the ground.

"What happens now?" Aaron asked when it looked as though all of the cells had been searched and there was no sign of them opening back up.

Jones shrugged. "They found a couple of shanks. And a cell phone. Now we stay on lock down until they get sick of the smell."

"Smell?"

"There's no showers on lock down, and this place is hot. Give it a day or two and you'll know what I mean."

It made sense. Aaron hoped the guards got sick pretty quickly. Although the other prisoners scared him, being in the yard and working with the crew was the only bit of normalcy he had left. He thought he would go mad locked in the tiny cell for too long.

"You got a girl?" Jones asked.

Aaron shrugged. "I don't know anymore."

"What do you mean you don't know?"

"I was dating a girl. Charity. She's a great girl. I was going to ask her to marry me. I went to ask her father's permission and I found him dead. They arrested me for his murder. I haven't heard from her since. She was at court the day I was sentenced. I tried to catch her eye, but she wouldn't even look at me."

"That's rough," Jones commented.

"Yeah, it is," Aaron agreed.

"Do you think she'll turn up for visitation on Friday assuming we're out of lock down?"

"I don't think so. Her mother would never allow her to visit a prison."

"Her mother wouldn't allow it? Dude, how old is she?"

Jones looked at him in obvious disgust.

"She's twenty. That's two years younger than me. It's different where I'm from, you know. We don't have the freedom of non-Amish people."

Jones looked confused now, which was better than disgust Aaron figured.

"I don't get it," Jones said. "Why don't you just leave?"

"It's all I've ever known," Aaron said. "And it's not so bad. Generally, we live happy fulfilling lives. Sometimes it goes wrong though obviously."

"Yeah obviously," Jones said. "You should write to her. You never know, she might write back even if she can't come."

"Maybe I will," Aaron said. He wanted to speak to Charity more than anything, but he was afraid. If he didn't reach out to her, he could convince himself she wanted to see him but her mother wouldn't allow it. If he reached out to her and she rejected him, it would be more than he could bear. He held out very little hope that she would even speak to him. She thought he had killed her father after all.

Aaron didn't want to talk about Charity any more. He was worried he wouldn't be able to keep his emotions in check, and the last thing he needed was to be crying in front of the other prisoners. It would be like signing his own death warrant.

"What about you?" he asked Jones. "Have you got a girlfriend?"

"I've got a wife," Jones answered smiling. "She's the most beautiful woman in the world. We'd been married just over two years when I ended up here."

"Does she visit?"

"Sure. She knows I only did what I had to do to try and give her a better life, you know. The life she deserves. I swear if I miss my conjugal because of this stupid lock down I'll go nuts."

Jones's words gave Aaron something to think on. His wife was standing by him. That's what a wife should do, that's what he had always been taught at home. Couples stick together. They support each other through the good times and the bad. But the people who had taught him that had never been accused of killing anyone. Not least the father of the person they referred to.

Aaron asked himself, not for the first time, how this had happened. How he had come to be here. He was a good man. His faith was strong and he worked hard. Why him? Why was he being punished in this manner?

His only conclusion was that God was testing him. That must be it. God was seeing if he was strong enough and worthy enough to marry Charity. She deserved only the best, and he had to show that he was that man.

He wasn't sure how he would be able to do it from prison, but he knew he was going to give it his all. He would show her, with God as his witness. Maybe Jones was right. He should write to her, explain the truth of the situation and ask her forgiveness.

CHAPTER 3

"I need you to cover for me tomorrow," Charity whispered to Rebecca on Thursday evening as the two young women walked home from the fields.

"What are you up to?" Rebecca asked.

"You said you didn't want to be involved."

"I don't, but I want to know where you'll be. I need to know you're safe."

"I'm going to visit him in prison."

"What? You can't do that. Your mother would never forgive you if she found out."

"She won't find out though will she?"

"Not from me, but people talk Charity. It's hard to have secrets around here. It's not our way."

"It's a risk I have to take."

"How will you even get there? It's a long way on the bus."

"Do you remember Noah who grew up along the road?"

"Noah who left the village?"

"Yeah. We still keep in touch. He's picking me up and bringing me some clothes to wear."

"What's wrong with your usual clothes?"

"He said it would draw attention to me. And you said it yourself. People talk. Mother would be much more likely to somehow find out if there where whispers about one of the Amish people turning up for prison visitation."

"Is there anything I can say to talk you out of this?" Rebecca asked with very little hope that she could.

"No," Charity said with finality.

"Then good luck," she said. "You're going to need it."

* * *

JONES STOOD up as the cell door opened. He walked to the opening and stepped through, looking back at Aaron.

"Keep it moving Jones," snapped Benson. "Yoder, move it."

Aaron jumped up and followed Jones out of the cell.

"I think there's been a mistake," he said to Benson. "I'm not expecting anyone."

"Sort it out with the COs down there," Benson snapped. "I'm not you messenger."

Aaron shrugged and kept walking, trying not to get his hopes up. It had to be a mistake. His mother would never come here and Charity certainly wouldn't. Maybe it was his lawyer he reasoned.

They made their way through the prison, stopping at various cells to collect other inmates.

"Wait here," Benson ordered when they reached the visitation room. He consulted his clip board. "Jones, Platt, you two have conjugals today. You know the drill."

"I hope it's your girl," Jones said to Aaron with a grin as he made his way with Platt down a corridor to their right.

"Remember the rules inmates. No touching, no shouting. Any sign of a disturbance and you go to seg. Am I making myself clear?"

The inmates chorused "Yes."

Aaron wasn't entirely clear what seg was, but he had a feeling he wouldn't want to find out.

Benson pushed a door open and the inmates filed through. Aaron was last in line. When he reached the door, Benson put his arm across it.

"You see anyone you know inmate?" Benson asked.

Aaron's eyes scanned the room. He was so intent on spotting his lawyer, he almost missed her. His eyes darted back to her. He couldn't believe she was here. Charity.

"Yes boss. My girlfriend is here," he responded.

"How sweet," said Benson sarcastically. He removed his arm. "Remember the rules Yoder."

Aaron nodded without looking back. He couldn't take his eyes off Charity. She was a picture of beauty. It was strange seeing her dressed in jeans and a modest blouse, but she would still be beautiful to him if she was wrapped in a garbage bag.

He approached the table she sat at.

"I didn't expect you to come here," he said as he sat down. He went to pull the chair in towards the table a little and noticed it was bolted to the floor.

"I didn't expect to be here," she said. Her face creased with concern when she looked at his face properly. "What happened? Who did that to you?"

His hand moved absently to the cut on his lip. "We had a lock down, where you can't leave your cell. When we were allowed out, there was a rush for the shower. Someone decided the new guy doesn't get to go before him, even if he was there first."

Her eyes filled with tears. "It's ok. It's nothing," he said.

"It's not just that. It's everything. Seeing you here."

He shrugged. "It's all part of God's plan I guess. What are you doing here Charity? Does your mother know where you are?"

"Of course not. And she's not going to find out. No one from home knows I'm here except Rebecca."

"How did you get here?"

"Noah brought me. Aaron, none of that's important. I want to talk about you."

"Ok," Aaron said. This was the part where she broke his heart. He steeled himself.

"Why did you plead guilty to something you hadn't done?"

He hadn't expected that. He had expected her to accuse him of killing her father, call him a few terrible names and leave.

He thought for a second. "Honestly, I don't know. My lawyer was giving me all of this information. He said I would almost certainly be found guilty if it went to trial, and I would be looking at a life sentence, or even the death penalty. He said he could get me a deal. I would do fifteen years. It didn't sound so bad until I got here. I don't know if I can do it Charity."

Her eyes glistened with unshed tears.

"Can't you appeal?"

"No. I wasn't sure, but I talked to Jones. My cell mate. He said I could appeal the length of the sentence, but not the actual case. You can't appeal being found guilty when you said it yourself."

"Are you going to appeal the sentence?"

He shook his head. "My lawyer advised against it. He said it was possible they would add extra time rather than take some off. He thinks I got off lightly."

"How is fifteen years for something you didn't do getting off lightly?" A single tear ran down Charity's cheek. She brushed it away angrily.

"I've done some research. Often, when you are offered a plea bargain, it's because the prosecution has a weak case, and they aren't confident they will win. They can't have had much evidence because you didn't do it."

Aaron shrugged. "It's too late to worry about that now. I can torture myself knowing I shouldn't have taken the deal, or I can let it go and just concentrate on doing my time and getting out of here."

"I was in the court room you know. On the day you were sentenced."

"I know. I wanted so badly to speak to you, but I couldn't. You wouldn't even look at me," he finished quietly.

"I'm sorry," Charity said. "I was a mess. I didn't know what to think. I didn't believe it for a second, but then to hear you say you were guilty. Anyway, that's when I started doing a bit of digging and learned about plea bargains. I was hoping that was what this is."

"Is that when you knew I hadn't done it?"

"A part of me knew from the moment you were accused you hadn't done it. The rest of me had doubts. I'm sorry, but that's the truth."

"It's ok," Aaron said. "I understand why you had doubts."

"I came here today because I wanted to see you, and because I did still have a small doubt. I don't anymore. Just seeing you in here makes me see that it's not you, and your words confirmed it."

"Thank you," Aaron said. He felt a huge burden lifted from his shoulders. He could do this if she just believed in him.

"I'm going to find out what really happened here Aaron. I'm getting you out of here."

"No," Aaron said. "It could be dangerous."

"I didn't come here to argue with you," Charity said firmly. "I came here to tell you what I am planning."

Aaron realised he couldn't do anything to stop her. He didn't like it, not one bit, but Charity had always been head strong. When she had a cause, there was no stopping her. He was grateful she was on his side, but that wouldn't stop him worrying about her.

"What's it like in here?" she asked.

"Like Hell," Aaron responded honestly.

CHAPTER 4

Charity sat in silence as the car moved along at a slow pace. They had hit the rush hour traffic and were getting nowhere fast.

"Are you ok? You haven't said more than two words since you came out of there," Noah said, breaking Charity's thoughts.

"Huh? Sorry. I was in a world of my own. Can I ask you a huge favour?"

"Even huger that driving you to the prison and back?"

"Yes,"

"Relax. That was a joke. Ask away."

"Can I stay with you for a couple of weeks?"

"Where's this coming from Charity? You have never shown the slightest interest in leaving the order."

"I'm not leaving the order. Well, not by choice anyway. I might find myself removed, but it's a risk I will have to take. Is that a yes?"

"It's a maybe. I want to know what's going on first."

She nodded. He was right. He had a right to know what was going on if she was to stay with him.

"I lied to you about my reasons for coming here today. I'm sorry. I didn't come here to face my father's killer and get closure. I came here today because a very large part of me believed Aaron was innocent and I had to talk to him. I am convinced now."

Noah's eyes widened. "You really believe that?"

"I really do," Charity responded.

"You know, if you'd told me that I still would have brought you. Now let me guess. You want to stay with me because you don't want your mother poking about in your business while you try to find a way to prove Aaron's innocent."

"How did you know?" Charity asked. It was her turn to be surprised.

"Because I know you Charity. I know what you're like when you find a cause. Yes. You can stay with me."

"Thank you," she said. "Really. Thank you. I need to stop at a payphone."

"Whatever you say," laughed Noah.

* * *

CHARITY CLIMBED INTO THE CAR, tears running down her cheeks.

"It didn't go well I take it?" Noah said, handing her a tissue.

She took it and wiped her eyes.

"Actually, it went better than I'd hoped."

"So why the tears?"

"I feel guilty for lying to my mother," she said. "She thinks I'm spending some time with my brother. I told her my father's death had made me question my faith and I need some time away to get perspective. That's why I needed to stop at a phone yesterday. I called my brother and got him to agree to cover for me if my mother does get in touch with him"

Noah considered her words. "I can understand the guilt, but you did the right thing Charity. If you'd told her the truth, she would have only worried."

Charity nodded. She knew the rest as well. The words he had carefully left unspoken. If she had told the truth, she would have been cast out, disowned and she would never be able to go back. This way, she had a chance.

"The first thing I need to do…"

Noah interrupted her. "The first thing you need to do is get some clothes. If you want anyone official to take you seriously, you need real world clothes."

"I don't have any money," she said quietly.

"It's a good job I do then," Noah said with a grin. "Where does Rebecca think you are?"

"She knows the truth but she will stick to the cover story."

"I hope you're right," he said.

CHAPTER 5

Charity awoke early as always. Even at this hour, there was traffic on the streets. She could hear it from where she lay in Noah's spare room.

She crossed to the window and looked out at the street. There were cars by the dozen, and people jogging, walking dogs and hurrying to work. It was a different world out here.

Charity felt scared, she had no idea how this world worked, or what her place in it could be. She knew she couldn't let her fear stop her.

She moved back from the window and fell to her knees at the bedside. She recited the Lord's Prayer and then she told God all her fears and prayed for His strength and guidance. She felt better when she was done praying, peaceful.

She reminded herself of why she was here. What she was doing was important, bigger than her fear. She had God on her side, she was sure of that.

She got dressed in the strange clothes. It was surreal to her to open a wardrobe and find she had a choice. She had no real idea about what would work as an outfit, and she was glad Noah had advised her.

She had ended up with two pairs of jeans and half a dozen plain t-shirts in various colours along with a pair of sneakers. She also had a pants suit and heeled court shoes. That was what she should wear for official meetings Noah had told her.

She wasn't sure if visiting Aaron's lawyer counted as an official meeting, but she had a feeling it did. She looked at herself in the mirror and smiled. It was like looking at someone else.

She had drawn the line at make-up. God would forgive her the clothes, they were necessary she had figured, but painting her face was going too far.

She was on her own today, Noah had gone to work. She would have to make her own way to the lawyer's office and talk to him herself.

She carried the shoes downstairs and left them by the door. After a quick drink of water, she made her way to the door and pulled it open. She was assaulted with noise. It was so loud she almost pushed the door shut again.

She berated herself. It was no louder than it had been on Friday when she had gone to the prison to visit Aaron. It just felt strange being alone.

She slipped her feet into the shoes and stepped out. She checked the handbag she now carried. The keys and cash Noah had given her were there. And the make shift map he had drawn her of how to get to the lawyer's office. That was all she would need.

She pulled the door closed and set off. She had barely reached the gate when she stumbled and turned her ankle.

She bent down and massaged it. She missed her flat, sensible shoes already. She stood back up and stumbled along. The shoes were painful. They rubbed the backs of her ankles and pinched her toes. The balls of her feet burned. Why did women do this to themselves by choice she wondered.

She reached the bus stop and stood waiting, switching her weight from foot to foot. She didn't have long to wait until the bus came. With a quick glance at her map, she got on.

"Milton Street please," she said, handing the driver a five-dollar bill.

He gave her her change and a ticket. She moved down the bus and sat down. That wasn't so bad she reasoned. It had been easy, and the driver hadn't looked her like she was weird. It gave her the confidence to believe she could do this.

She watched through the window as the bus drove along, stopping along the way to let people on and off. Somewhere along the way, she felt her fear turn to excitement. She was free, even if it was only for a week or two. The possibilities were endless.

She felt the guilt at rejoicing in her freedom. She was here because Aaron's freedom had been taken away.

With a jolt, she saw the street sign for Milton Street. She jumped to her feet and made her way to the door of the bus.

It pulled up and the doors opened. "Thank you," she called to the driver as she stepped carefully down, her feet screaming at her.

She consulted her map. The law firm should be just at the end of this block. She set off walking. She wanted nothing more than to remove the shoes and maybe burn them, but she didn't have to be from the city to know that wouldn't be appropriate.

She finally found herself outside the law firm's office. She double checked she had the right building. Maddison and Healy. That was the one, she was in the right place.

She pushed the glass door open and entered a cool reception area. She approached the desk.

"My name is Charity Troyer. I have an appointment with Mr Maddison," she said.

"Go on up. He's expecting you. First floor and to the right."

"Thank you."

Charity hobbled up the stairs and went to the right. She spotted a door with James Maddison and a bunch of letters that meant nothing to her on the window. She knocked gently.

"Come in," he called. She entered. "Have a seat Miss Troyer. What can I do for you?"

Now she was here, she wasn't sure where to start.

"I...I," she stammered. She took a breath and started again. "I'm here about Aaron Yoder."

Maddison looked at her questioningly. He was expecting more. She fought to get her thoughts in order.

"Aaron's innocent and I need your help to prove it," she finally said.

Maddison continued to stare at her.

"Miss Troyer, I don't know exactly what your interest is in this case, but I can assure you that isn't true. Mr Yoder pleaded guilty. You were there in the court. You know it to be true."

"My interest is twofold Mr Maddison," Charity said, her nerves gone. His scepticism had broken the spell. "Firstly, I would like to find out who really killed my father and see justice done. Secondly, I would like my boyfriend exonerated. He accepted a plea bargain on your recommendation without knowing enough of the facts to see what a terrible choice that was."

Maddison's expression finally changed. She had caught him off guard. He mentally kicked himself. He should have connected the name of this woman with the name of the victim in the case. It's not like it was exactly a common name.

"Miss Troyer, I understand your frustration, but I really don't appreciate you coming in here and insulting my work."

"And I really don't like you getting an innocent man to spend fifteen years in prison."

Maddison had underestimated the woman. She had entered like a nervous poodle. Now she seemed more like a bear.

"Look, I think we got off on the wrong foot. Let's start over. Why do you think Mr Yoder is innocent?"

"I know Aaron," Charity said. "He is a religious man, hard working. He's no murderer. It's not something he would even consider. Even the prosecution knew that – their case was weak. They don't offer plea bargains to murderers Mr Maddison. Not unless they know there's a good chance the evidence won't stick in court."

Maddison laughed. "You have certainly done your research Miss Troyer. You actually raise a very good point about the prosecution. But I have seen their evidence. It's not something that would be easy to explain away. I'm not sure what else to tell you."

"What evidence did they claim to have?"

"It's not a claim. They had it."

"Ok. Can I see it?"

"I really shouldn't do this," Maddison said. He stood up and went to a large filing cabinet. "But I have a feeling you won't give up on this. Maybe once you see the evidence, you will accept Yoder's guilt and move on with your life."

Charity went to argue then decided to let him think whatever he wanted as long as she got to see that file.

Maddison sat back down and opened the file. He spread the papers around and motioned her to come to his side of the desk so she could see.

She did. He pointed to a section and paraphrased it for her.

"Yoder was found standing over your father's body with the murder weapon still on the scene."

"Wouldn't it make sense for him to leave the scene and hide the weapon if he was in fact guilty?"

"It would, but sometimes the shock of killing affects people."

"Is that the only evidence? He happened to be there?" Charity was incredulous. "What was his motive supposed to be?"

"You don't need a motive when there is physical evidence. Especially when the accused admits their guilt. What other reason would he have had for being in your father's office before it was open?"

"I don't know, but it seems a bit of a stretch to assume someone is a killer because they were in someone's office before it was open. Was there any signs of forced entry?"

Maddison flicked further into the file. "No. But it was established that your father knew the accused. It was accepted that he opened the door for him, and then things took a violent turn."

"Aaron must have given a statement when he was first arrested. What was in the statement? What did he say happened?"

"It doesn't matter. His statement was tossed out as a fabrication when he pleaded guilty."

"I'd like to see it all the same."

Maddison flicked further into the file.

He scanned through the statement. "He claims he was visiting your father to ask his permission to request your hand in marriage. He said when he got there, your father was already dead."

Charity didn't know how to feel about that. She was ecstatic that he had wanted to marry her, but she was also sad. If he hadn't gone to her father when he did, he would still be free. She felt strangely guilty.

"He claims he didn't leave the scene because he panicked. Now that, I can believe, but why wouldn't he call 911? We were alerted to the crime hours later when a client of your father arrived at his office. He saw Yoder still standing over the body. He fled and called us."

"If he didn't leave the scene, he couldn't call 911," Charity explained. "We're Amish. We don't have cell phones."

"Surely there would be a phone in the office though?"

"Yes, of course, but Aaron wouldn't have been able to use it." Charity saw Maddison's frown. "It's hard to explain to anyone who isn't Amish. The business's telephone line was only to be used for the business. That's it. It really is that black and white to our people."

As Charity spoke, her eyes wandered to the opposite page. The coroner's report on her father. She winced, but her eyes were drawn to it. She scanned over the more gruesome details. Her eyes settled on something and it was like a light switched on in her head.

"Forget that for a second. What time did Aaron say he arrived at the office?"

Maddison went back to the beginning of the statement. "8.30am."

"Now look here," Charity said. "The coroner's report. It says the time of death was between four and five am."

Maddison nodded agreement. "Yes. It was assumed that Yoder lied about the time he arrived at the office."

"Assumed?" Charity asked coldly.

"Yes," confirmed Maddison. "These points you are raising are all points I would have looked into had the case gone to trial. However, it is my legal duty to present my clients with any deal offered, and to give them my honest assessment of their situation. The fact remains that

Yoder was looking at a life sentence, if not death row. Fifteen years was a good deal. When he gets out, he'll still be young enough to have a chance at a life."

"I'm not saying you purposely misled him. I'm merely saying you didn't do your job thoroughly. You should have looked into this before you advised Aaron to take the deal. How could you provide an honest assessment when you didn't even know the facts?"

"It's just the way it works. I am duty bound to represent so many clients per year pro bono. That means for free. Ultimately though, I have to dedicate the majority of my time to paying clients. That's how I make a living. When Yoder told me he wanted to take the deal, I wasn't about to argue with him."

Charity was raging inside, but she had to control it. She had never felt such anger before and it scared her a little.

She took several deep breaths before she trusted herself to speak again.

"Ok, fair enough. You're not bad at your job, you're just a terrible human being. Is that better?"

"It's probably more accurate. Now if you're done making accusations, I have work to attend to."

"Please," Charity said. "You have it all there in front of you. You know he's innocent. You know he panicked and took the plea bargain because you said he could end up being executed."

Maddison sighed. He didn't know what it was about this girl, but something about her touched him. Maybe it was the fact she believed in something, someone. Something he had never really done.

He sighed. "I'll look into it," he said finally, against his better judgement.

"Thank you," she told him. She wrote down Noah's cell phone number. "When you have something, I can be reached on this number."

CHAPTER 6

It was finally Friday. Visitation day. The last few days had felt like a year to Charity.

She was so excited to see Aaron, and she had a lot of questions for him. As yet, Maddison hadn't called, and she was starting to think that he had only agreed to look into the case to get rid of her.

She planned on going to see him again on Monday, but when she did, she would have something further. Something he couldn't ignore. She just didn't know what yet.

She sat in the visitation room, eagerly waiting for Aaron to come out. She was glad to be wearing the sneakers today. Her feet had been in such a mess when she had gotten back to Noah's after wearing the heels. They had been a mass of blisters and skinned patches.

The door opened and the inmates filed in. She spotted Aaron and waved him over.

He sat down opposite her and beamed at her.

"It's so good to see you," he said.

"You too," she responded, pleased to see there were no new cuts or bruises on his face.

"Aaron I need to ask you some things. About the day you found my father's body."

"Ok," he agreed. "Are you sure you want to hear about it. I know how much he meant to you."

"I need to Aaron. It's the only way to get you out of here and find out who really killed my father. You said you arrived at 8.30?"

He nodded.

"And the police report says there was no sign of forced entry?"

He nodded again. "When I got there, the front door was ajar. It hadn't been forced and I thought maybe your father had just not shut it hard enough for the lock to catch."

"My father was careful Aaron. He would have made sure that lock was secure. It was someone who had a key. Did you see anyone? Anyone at all when you were going to the office?"

"Only Mrs Schrock. You know, the cleaner from the office next to your father's?"

Charity knew exactly who he meant. She needed to speak to Mrs Schrock as soon as possible. The offices she cleaned shared a building with her father. Maybe she had seen someone. It must have been her who left the door ajar.

"Are you certain she's the only person you saw?"

"Yes. Totally certain," he said.

"Ok. That's great. Why didn't you tell the police you saw her?"

Aaron shrugged. "They didn't ask if I had saw anyone. I didn't think it was important. I figured they would know she had been there. She did work there after all."

"True," Charity said. She wasn't convinced the police had even spoken to Mrs Schrock. They had found their man, and they wouldn't want to find anything to suggest they were wrong.

They spent the rest of the visit talking about everyday life. Charity told him about life in the big city, and how she was getting used to it, but she missed her regular life. He told her about the latest project he was working on with the prison industries crew and he made her laugh out loud with a story of an inmate who had walked around in only his underwear for two days in protest to wearing the prison issue clothes.

The visit flew over and before they knew it, the guards were calling time.

They stood, and Aaron took Charity's hand and kissed her gently on the cheek. "Thank you Charity. I love you."

"I love you too," she said, her cheek tingling where he had kissed her.

"Move it along," a CO ordered as the inmates said their goodbyes.

Charity left the prison and walked towards the bus stop. She was deep in thought, trying to work out a way to go and see Mrs Schrock without her mother finding out.

It just wasn't possible. Maybe she could find a way to talk to Rebecca and see if she would talk to Mrs Schrock for her. She didn't want to have to involve Rebecca, but she could see no other way. Noah wasn't an option. Mrs Schrock would never talk to an outsider.

She didn't notice the car pull up beside her until she heard Noah's voice.

"Charity, get in," he called.

She jumped a little then made her way around the car and got into the passenger seat.

"What are you doing here? I thought you were at work?"

"I was," Noah said, his voice barely containing his excitement. "I took a half day. Maddison called. He said there's been a break through. He wants to talk to you right away."

"Did he say what it was about?"

"No. He wouldn't give me any details."

CHAPTER 7

Charity jumped from the car the second Noah parked it. She hopped impatiently from foot to foot as she waited for him to get out. They hurried across the parking lot.

Charity didn't even stop at the reception desk, she just called her name as she headed for the stairs. It must be something big, something important if Maddison wouldn't discuss it with Noah.

She knocked on his office door and opened it without waiting for a response.

"Miss Troyer. Good to see you again. Please, sit down."

His eyes darted to Noah and she realised she hadn't introduced him. "This is my friend, Noah," she said. "What have you found out?"

"Something about this case has niggled me for a while if I'm completely honest, but it was closed as far as I was concerned. A done deal if you will. Then you showed up.

I did intend on looking into it as I said I would, although whether or not you believed that, I'm not sure.

"I finally found a spare hour this morning. I reviewed the case file, not really expecting to find anything I didn't already know about. But I was found something. The murder weapon. The hammer that was found on the scene?

"When I looked back over the lab report, it confirms that Yoder's prints were on it. He didn't deny touching it. He said he picked it up. That was a stupid move, one I didn't believe he had made until now. The lab reports show some unidentified prints too. We could just have found us a suspect."

Charity was speechless for a second.

"Thank you," she finally managed. She remembered what Aaron had told her. "There's something else. Someone might have seen something."

Maddison waited for her to finish.

"I spoke to Aaron this morning. He saw Mrs Schrock on the morning he went to the office. He didn't mention it to the police, because he thought they would know she had been there. She's the cleaner in the office opposite my father's. They share a front door. Maybe she left it open by accident. Or maybe she saw someone."

"Schrock you say? How do you spell that?"

Charity spelled it out for him. "I'm going to go and talk to her when we leave here."

"No," Maddison said. "You can't be involved." He held up a hand and cut off her protest. "If you want anything she says to be admissible in court you can't get involved."

"Ok," Charity reluctantly agreed. "She's old and very set in her ways. I'm not sure she'll talk to an outsider."

"I can be pretty charming when I have to be. She'll talk. I will call you as soon as I have anything further. Promise me you won't go and try to talk to Mrs Schrock."

"I promise," Charity said. She believed Maddison would look into this properly now he had something. And she could always talk to Mrs Schrock later if Maddison couldn't get her to talk. She couldn't imagine him being charming.

CHAPTER 8

It was Saturday morning. Not even a full day since she had spoken to Maddison, and already she was restless. She sat down then stood back up again. She paced the room. Then sat back down again and repeated the process.

She had been doing it for the last hour. Noah had tried to persuade her to go out somewhere with him, but she said no. She wanted to be ready to leave at a moment's notice if Maddison called.

"I'm going to make some coffee. Do you want a cup?" Noah said standing up.

She shook her head. "No thanks. I'm jittery enough."

As he left the room, his cell phone rang. They looked at each other and Noah crossed the room and snatched it up.

"Hello?"

"Why?"

"Ok, we'll be there."

He hung up. It was frustrating only hearing one end of the conversation.

"What?" Charity said as Noah reached for his keys.

"Maddison wants us to meet him at the prison as soon as we can get there. I don't know anything else."

Charity had a hundred questions, but none of them were questions Noah would be able to answer so she kept them to herself.

The main thing that kept going through her mind was that Aaron must have been hurt or worse. Why else would his lawyer have been called? And why would he want her there?

They finally arrived at the prison. Noah parked the car and they got out. They headed towards the door.

"Miss Troyer, over here." Charity span around. Maddison was just getting out of his car.

"What's going on?" she asked as they hurried over to him. "Is Aaron ok?"

"Why don't you ask him yourself?" Maddison smiled as his passenger door opened and Aaron stepped out.

Charity felt herself burst into happy tears. She ran to him and he wrapped his arms around her. She clung to him.

"Thank you," He whispered into her hair. She squeezed him tighter.

When she thought she had herself under control enough to speak she pulled back.

"What happened?"

"After our chat yesterday, I went to the business opposite your father's. I wanted to talk to the owner about Mrs Schrock. He couldn't tell me much. He just said she was good at her job and that's all he needed to know. On my way out, I spotted a cleaning supplies cupboard. It wasn't locked and I managed to lift a couple of prints.

"I sent them to be analysed and they were a match for the partial on the murder weapon. I called the prosecution lawyer and updated her and together we went to the judge.

"I told him everything, and Miranda, the prosecution lawyer confirmed it all. She applied for Aaron's immediate release and exoneration and an arrest warrant for Evelyn Schrock.

"The judge granted us both. Mrs Schrock has been arrested. She broke down at the station and made a full confession. Your father was responsible for her husband's estate when he died. His will stated that she was to get nothing. It was all to go to various charities.

"Needless to say, this displeased her somewhat. She decided your father was responsible. The anger ate at her until one morning, she took a hammer into work with her and killed your father with it.

"It explains why the door was left ajar – she didn't want to be the chief suspect. It also explains why there was no sign of a struggle. Your father wouldn't have had a reason to feel in danger."

He turned to Aaron with a smile. "What it still doesn't explain, is why you were stupid enough to touch the murder weapon. A word of advice. If you ever find yourself in the middle of a crime scene again, touch nothing."

Aaron laughed. "Understood," he said. He shook hands with Maddison. "Thank you. For everything."

"It's not me you need to thank, but I suspect you know that already."

"What happens now?" Charity asked.

"You go home and live your lives. Aaron has been completely exonerated of any wrong doing, and your father's killer is safely behind bars, where she will remain for a very long time."

Maddison said his goodbyes and drove away.

"Will you take us home?" Charity asked Noah.

"Of course. By home do you mean my place or home home."

"Home home," she said. "I've got a lot of explaining to do,"

They got into Noah's car. Noah and Aaron chatted. Noah had a lot of questions about prison, which Aaron seemed happy enough to answer.

"You two know each other right?" Charity suddenly asked.

"Yeah," laughed Aaron.

CHAPTER 9

Noah drove away and left Charity and Aaron on the corner.

"You should go talk to your parents. Tell them what's happened," Charity said. "Come over when you're done. If I'm not welcome back home, I'll wait for you here."

He nodded, but he seemed reluctant to leave her. She smiled. "Go. We'll be together soon."

She reached her home and pushed the door open.

"Mother, I'm home," she called.

Her mother rushed out of the kitchen. Her apron was covered with flour which ended up all down Charity's front as they hugged. She didn't care.

"Let me go change into my real clothes and then I have a lot to tell you."

"The clothes can wait. I have a lot to tell you too. Does this mean you're home for good?"

Charity nodded.

"Evelyn Schrock was arrested for your father's murder. Aaron is being released from prison. He was innocent all along."

Charity hung her head. "I know."

"How?"

"Mother, I must ask your forgiveness. I lied to you. I have been staying with a friend in the city. I have been working alongside Aaron's lawyer to prove his innocence, and to get justice for my father."

"Oh Charity. How could I not forgive you? But I must ask. Why did you not feel you could come to me with the truth?"

"I don't know. I thought you would try to stop me."

"Maybe I would have," her mother answered, "but if you could convince a lawyer to reopen a closed case, I'm sure you could have convinced me of the truth of your words."

"I hadn't considered that. I'm sorry Mother."

"You're forgiven. In my eyes and the eyes of our Lord I'm sure."

"Thank you," Charity said, hugging her again. "Mother, the day father died, Aaron was going to him to ask his permission to propose to me. So much has happened since then. Do you think he will still ask? And if he does, will I have your blessing to accept?"

"I do think he will still ask, and of course you will have my blessing," she smiled. "Now, tell me, what did you make of the big city?"

Charity considered the question. "It was scary at first, but I got used to it. It's very different to the way we live."

"That it is. Are you tempted to leave here?"

"No," Charity answered. "I would like to go and visit Noah every so often, but I'm not tempted to live there. I missed everyone too much. More than that, I missed out simple way of life. Everything is so complicated outside of the village."

Her mother nodded. "Yes, our way is much simpler. I'm happy that you are happy here. Now, why don't you go and change. I have a feeling Aaron will be by soon, and you want him to see you as you are."

Charity did as her mother suggested. She expected her old plain clothes to feel strange to her now, but they didn't. They felt like her. Like coming home.

She was just leaving the bedroom when she heard a knock at the door. She came into the main room at the same time as Aaron and his parents.

"It seems they already knew the whole story when I arrived," Aaron said.

Charity laughed. "Word spreads quickly. My mother knew too."

"Sit down," Charity's mother said. Aaron's parents sat down. Charity and her mother followed suit. Aaron remained standing.

"What's wrong?" Charity asked him. He appeared suddenly nervous.

He ignored her question. "Charity, the day your father was killed, I was going to see him to get his permission to ask for your hand in marriage. I'm sure you know that now. I was too late, but I hope he is watching us and sees how happy we are together. I hope he would have granted me his permission."

He stopped and looked at Charity's mother. "He would have. He thought very highly of you," she said.

Aaron nodded his thanks to her. He knelt before Charity and took her hand in his.

"I guess what I'm trying to say is Charity, I love you. More than I can begin to explain right now. Will you do me the honour of agreeing to be my wife?"

Charity's eyes filled with tears. She had cried a lot these last few weeks, but today, the only tears she had shed had been happy tears.

"Yes," she said simply.

Amish Investigation

LOVES PLAIN TRUTHS

Amish Investigation

CHAPTER 1 - ONLY CHILD

"Sometimes I envy you, Leah Miller," Grace said as she flopped across her friend's bed. "You have a bedroom all to yourself, you've never had to wear hand me downs, and you don't have a dozen *shveshtahs* and *bruders* who all want to get in the bathroom at the same time. Being an only child must be wonderful."

Leah turned and stared incredulously at her friend. The two girls had grown up next door to each other in the Amish community of Serenity Falls and Leah had always yearned to be like Grace and other Amish children, most of who came from large families. It wasn't unusual for an Amish couple to have ten or more *kinner*. Grace herself was one of 13.

"Are you serious, Grace? Don't you know how lucky you are to have such a big, happy family? There were many times growing up, and still are actually, when I'm just plain lonely. I'd love to have readymade playmates and some sisters to share the work around here. It's a lot for me and *Maemm* to handle. *Daett* too, could use some sons to help him with the farm. And you must have so much fun. There are always plenty of people for volleyball or to play board games with."

"I suppose you're right. I do love them all but sometimes they are so noisy, you can't hear yourself think." Grace pondered it for a moment then made a face. "I still can't imagine what it would be like to have a whole room to yourself, though."

Leah laughed and joined Grace on the mattress. "Okay, I'll give you that one. Hey, are you planning on going to the party at the Walker's house Friday?" The Walkers were an English family who lived in a spacious brick house on the outskirts of town.

"I am. I'm going to wear tight blue jeans and an off-the-shoulder red sweater. How about you?"

Because they were Amish, it was not often in their lives the two girls would dress like Englishers. Only during *Rumspringa*, the running around time between the ages of 16 and until they married or decided to become baptized, could they indulge in the ways of outsiders and shed their traditional dresses and *kappas* in favor of more stylish clothing and enjoy a taste of worldly ways.

"I haven't decided yet," Leah admitted, a blush stealing up her cheeks. "I know I want it to be something special. Something that will catch Luke Troyer's eye."

"So that's the way the wind blows is it, Leah? Well, I can't say as I blame you. He's one fine looking carpenter. And, he doesn't seem to have taken a shine to anyone special yet since he came to live here a few months ago. Though if I remember right I did see you two talking together at the singing after church Sunday last week."

Leah's cheeks took on an even brighter hue, contrasting sharply with her corn silk colored hair and turquoise eyes.

"I think he's about the nicest man I've ever met," she confessed. "He came to help his aunt after his uncle Jeb was paralyzed from that fall he took off a roof last spring. Since Jeb and Sarah have seven daughters, none of whom are married yet, they really needed some masculine help. He says he likes it here and plans on staying."

"I bet you were happy to hear that," Grace giggled and winked at her best friend. "That gives you time to set your trap."

"Oh, you, enough silly talk." Leah threw a pillow at the still lounging Grace. "Let's go snitch some cookies and milk before you have to go home."

Leah woke bright and early the next morning as usual. She was headed downstairs before the rooster finished crowing. Not to her surprise, though, she found *Maemm* already in the kitchen, coffee on the stove and bacon sizzling in a cast iron skillet.

"*Gut* morning, *Dochtah*," Ruth Miller greeted her only child, a happy smile creasing her apple cheeks. "*Daett* is in the barn. Lady's puppies are coming. He thought you would like to come and see."

"Oh, *jah*, *Maemm*, I'd love to see the newborns. But don't you need my help with breakfast?"

"You go on, Leah. I can handle this alone today. It's a special day, after all. Not every day do we get new puppies."

"*Danka, Maemm*," she called over her shoulder as she grabbed a shawl to ward off the early morning chill and ran towards the barn. She pulled open the big wooden door and stepped in, spotting her father kneeling in a stall nearby.

"Ach, Leah," he greeted her. "Come see the two fine new collie pups we have. And there's more on the way."

Leah went and knelt in the straw by her father and Lady lifted her head and managed to wag her tail one time in greeting before refocusing on the birth of the next puppy.

Leah stroked the silky head of the panting dog and cooed encouraging words to her. Like Leah's own mother, Lady was giving birth late in life. For some reason she had never become pregnant until now at the ripe old doggie age of six years.

An odd thought popped into her head as she watched another pup squirm into the world. Lady immediately began tending to it, knowing instinctively what to do for her baby.

"Don't you wish people could be like dogs, *Daett*? Then Maemm could have had a whole litter of babies instead of just one."

A chuckle rumbled from Amos Miller's throat, making his beard shake with laughter. "*Ach, dochtah*, you do have quite the imagination. You always have. But your mother and I were thrilled to have you, our only child. We had nearly given up hope of becoming parents. We've told you before we never even revealed your mother was expecting you, we'd been disappointed so many times before. When you finally came into our lives we were overjoyed. We knew *Gott* had blessed us with his finest gift, a child of our own."

"Oh, *Daett*, I'm the lucky one to have such loving parents."

"Besides," he added, "we know you will soon be blessing us with lots of grandchildren, *jah*?"

"Well, not too soon," she qualified his statement. "I don't even have a suitor yet."

"Not because men are not interested in you," he informed her, wagging his finger in her face. "I think you are being, what do they say, hard to get."

"No, *Daett*, I'm being particular. After all, it's hard to find someone who can live up to the fine example you've set as a good husband and father. I won't settle for less."

Amos studied his only child with loved filled brown eyes, a tender smile crossing his face.

"You never fail to make me happy you came into our lives, Leah." He patted on her back. "Well, Lady seems to be doing fine so I think we should go eat breakfast. What do you say?"

"I say I'm starving. Let's go."

CHAPTER 2 - CURIOSER AND CURIOSER

After a meal of bacon and eggs, blueberry muffins, and fresh from the garden cantaloupe, Leah hitched Hershey to the buggy and headed to town. She worked at the Crazy Quilt Shoppe, a small specialty store in Serenity Falls that sold Amish made quilts, quilting supplies, and quilted accessories such as throw pillows and handbags. Her friend and boss Sherry Harper owned the store and not only had a thriving business selling to the numerous tourists that came through the town but had a booming online clientele as well.

Leah loved her job. She was already an expert with a needle and a couple of her own quilts had sold for upwards of a thousand dollars. Not only that, Sherry was a great boss. Easygoing but with a shrewd head for business, she also had a great sense of humor.

The bell over the shop door jangled as Leah entered the store. Sherry, as usual, had arrived an hour previous, enjoying the quiet early morning time that allowed her to work on the books and marketing campaigns.

"*Gut* morning, Sherry. It's a beautiful day *Gott* has given us today, isn't it?" Leah slipped off her shawl and went to hang it and her bonnet in the backroom.

"Gorgeous," Sherry agreed. "Oh, by the way. There was a man here today looking for you. At least I think it was you."

"A man? Looking for me?" Leah knew she sounded like a mockingbird but she had no clue who Sherry could be talking about…unless…she blushed as an image of Luke Troyer passed through her mind. But of course he wouldn't come here looking for her. Silly thought.

"Yes, an Englishman." The slim redhead crossed her arms and a slight frown creased her brow. "He asked for a girl who was just about 18 and who went by the name of Miller. It sure sounded like you but I didn't tell him anything. I know Amish people like their privacy."

"Hmm, that's funny. Why would an Englisher be looking for me?"

"I don't know, honey, he didn't say."

Leah shrugged her shoulders. "It probably isn't even me he really wants. You know there are a boatload of Millers in Amish communities. Just because I'll be turning 18 in less than a month doesn't mean I'm the person he wants to find."

"I'm sure you're right, Leah." Sherry's pretty face still wore a worried expression. "Just be careful, okay?"

"Sure. Now let's forget him and get this day started."

The rest of the morning was busy. Leah taught a quilting class at ten while Sherry manned the front of the store. After class, Leah unpacked a shipment of batting and threads, putting each item in its place on the carefully organized shelves. By then her stomach was growling, demanding to be fed. Sherry had already gone to lunch and returned so Leah headed out around one o'clock.

Yoder's Café wasn't fancy but it did offer good home cooked meals and Leah had known the owner Mary Yoder since she'd been just a toddler. The woman was widowed now and was raising six children on her on.

When Leah walked in she noted most of the tables were full so she headed to the counter to find a seat on one of the worn black barstools.

"Afternoon, Leah," Mary Yoder greeted her. "What can I get you today?"

"I think I'll have a tenderloin and fries, Mary. Oh, and a lemon Coke, of course."

"Naturally. I know you love your lemon Cokes. Say, there was a man in here this morning asking questions. I think he was asking about you."

Leah's eyes grew round and she tilted her head quizzically. "An Englisher?"

"*Jah*. A guy about forty or so, wearing a polo shirt and khakis. How did you know?"

"Sherry told me the same guy was in the Crazy Quilt early this morning."

Now it was Mary's turn to look surprised. Her brows arched over faded blue eyes.

"Said he was looking for a girl named Miller who'd be turning 18 in the next couple weeks or so. Hey, won't you be eighteen in October? That's just around the corner."

"Yes, but I'm sure he's not looking for me. What possible reason could he have?"

Mary shrugged and turned to pass Leah's order into the kitchen.

"I don't know, Leah, but it sure sounded like he was talking about you."

Mary rushed away to take another order and left Leah alone to contemplate the question of the stranger making enquiries around town. She could think of no good reason why an English man would be looking for her. It must just be coincidence that the woman he sought was the same age as her and they shared the same last name.

Leah's food arrived and she made herself focus on the meal. As usual it was cooked perfectly and Leah made quick work of polishing it off. There was plenty to do when she got back to work so she didn't linger but waved goodbye to Mary and walked the two blocks back to the store.

The rest of the day flew by and Leah was too busy to think about the man again. By the end of the afternoon she was ready to go home and tackle her chores there. First, though, she'd promised *Maemm* she'd stop at the market and grab some cream of mushroom soup for the casserole she was making this evening.

Leah headed Hershey towards the edge of town and fastened the chocolate bay to the hitching post in the parking lot of Bennet's Market. This was a busy time of day for the grocery with harried working mothers rushing in to grab supplies they needed for supper. Leah got the soup and on impulse bought a bag of her mother's favorite chocolate candies. Ruth Miller had a sweet tooth and would be delighted with Leah's gift.

There was a line at the cash register but Bob Bennett never rushed a customer. He knew everyone in town and considered them all friends and always passed the time of day for a minute or two with each person who came to the checkout. Leah was familiar with his habit and waited patiently as he checked out the three people in front of her in line.

When it was her turn the grocer greeted her warmly as usual and asked about her parents.

"Glad to hear they're well, Miss Leah. Oh, say," he paused and pushed his glasses up his nose with a long bony finger. "By the way, there was a man in here today asking a lot of questions about where he could find a girl who sounds a lot like you."

CHAPTER 3 - MUM'S THE WORD

On the ride home Leah pondered whether to tell her parents about the man and his questions. Might they know anything about who it could be? Or would it just worry them that a strange man seemed to be looking for her?

Her intuition told her it would be the latter. Her parents had always tended to be a little overprotective of her, maybe because she was an only child and had come along so late in their lives. Probably best not to say anything unless something more developed.

Decision made, she turned Hershey onto the road that led to her family's farm. It also happened to be the same road where Luke Troyer lived with his aunt and uncle. She rarely caught a glimpse of him when she drove by but she always looked to see if he was in the yard.

Today must be her lucky day. Luke wasn't in the yard. Even better, he was mending a fence near the road. He heard the buggy approach and turned to wave then stepped to the roadside and motioned for her to stop.

She couldn't deny she enjoyed looking at him. Tall and muscular, Luke had a mop of curly dark hair and sparkling eyes the warm shade of spiced apple cider. Since he was still a bachelor he hadn't grown a beard yet so the twin dimples that flashed in his cheeks when he smiled were readily visible. He smiled a lot, she'd noticed, always cheerful and content with the world.

"*Gut* evening, Leah. On your way home from work?"

Leah blushed for no reason as he leaned against a nearby tree, arms crossed leisurely over his broad chest. Just his presence made her nerves tingle.

"*Jah*, it was a *gut* day." Oh, boy, for some reason she couldn't think of another word to say and blushed again.

"I'm glad. Will you give your father a message for me?" He ran his hand across his sweat dampened brow, his skin toasted golden brown from working in the sun every day. "Would you tell him I'll be able to start on that new storage shed he wants early next week after all? The garage I'm working on for the Bakers looks to be finished ahead of schedule. If I stay at it, it should be done by Friday."

Finally her brains started working again.

"I'll pass the word on. I'm sure he'll be pleased." She hesitated then took a bold step, at least bold for her. "You mentioned Friday. You know the Walker twins are having a birthday party that night? There's going to be a bonfire and S'mores and such. It will be a mix of English and Amish. Are you going?"

A broad smile broke out across his face. "I've been invited. If I get that job finished early enough and nothing comes up I'm planning on it. Especially if you're going to be there, Leah."

Okay, her brain shut down again. Her cheeks felt as red as ripe tomatoes. Why did this man make her speechless whenever he was around?

At last she managed to nod and croak, "I'll be there." Without another word she snapped the reins over Hershey's back, tossed Luke a wave goodbye and began the last leg of the journey home. She was irritated with herself. She was usually a good conversationalist but with Luke she couldn't think straight. He must think she hadn't a brain in her head.

Well, nothing she could do about it right now. Instead she'd think about what a beautiful autumn day it was and how happy she was to be home. She guided Hershey into the long drive that led up to the house. The trees were taking on their fall colors and the air smelled ripe with harvest. As the buggy crested the hill she saw *Daett* coming out of the barn followed by two or three barn cats and *Maemm* taking freshly laundered clothes off the line.

The sight of this happy place where she had grown up made her smile. Her parents hadn't heard her coming yet and she watched as *Daett* snuck up on *Maemm* and gave her a tight hug and a big kiss on the cheek. It warmed Lean's heart to see them together. She prayed she'd have a marriage as good as theirs someday. She might be an only child, but *Gott* had blessed her with the best parents on earth. Who was she to ask for more?

CHAPTER 4 - SOMEONE'S WATCHING

Leah stuck to her decision not to mention anything to her parents about the stranger asking questions about someone who may or may not be her. She wondered if the man was striking out blindly in a search for the woman he sought or if he had some information that had brought his hunt to Serenity Falls.

At any rate, she didn't hear any more about it the rest of the week and gradually he was pushed to the back of her mind. Her thoughts were more occupied by work. They were headed into a busy season with tourists flocking from the cities to enjoy the serenity of the autumn woods. Holiday orders for quilted tree skirts, stockings, ornaments, and other paraphernalia were coming in quickly. Things became so busy Sherry hired another two Amish women to assist them with meeting the demand.

Midweek after she got off work she met up with Grace and they hitched a ride with one of her English friends to the shopping mall in the county seat. It was rare that the two Amish women ventured into the center, but it was, after all, *rumspringa*, and they could have more adventures than usual.

The main purpose of their visit was to find something suitable for Leah to wear to the party Friday night. The two girls strolled through the mall, sometimes gawking at teenagers with rainbow colored hair and a multitude of piercings, other times staring into windows offering a myriad of fashions and other products.

"It's so hard to decide," Leah groaned. "This is all so different from what we're used to."

"Leah, that's what *rumspringa* is all about." Grace waved her hands as she talked. "Experiencing the difference so we can make an educated decision about what path we want to walk in the future."

"I know, Grace, but really, in my heart, I already know my decision. I love my church, love my family and our community. I can't imagine ever leaving it."

"I wish I was as sure as you," Grace retorted. "I want to get a taste for what the rest of the world is about. Then I'll make my decision. In the meantime, I'm going to have fun exploring my options. Now come on, let's go find you an outfit that will knock Luke Troyer's socks off."

Leah chuckled as her friend pulled her into a boutique that had a display of short dresses and tight jeans in the windows. Somehow she had a feeling the outfit she was looking for wouldn't be here.

AN HOUR later the girls were walking out of the mall, Leah clutching a sack that contained her treasures. They'd looked in several stores but finally, when they entered the fourth one, Leah saw exactly what she wanted.

It was a simple dress the same shade of periwinkle as her eyes. The soft fabric slid over her slender figure and highlighted all the right places. It had a square neck outlined with embroidered violets and a raised waistline that settled right below her breasts. The skirt ended a couple inches above her knees and showed off her long legs. The pair of beige flats she'd chosen to go with the dress kept it feeling casual and she even indulged in a tiny gold cross necklace. Jewelry was forbidden to the Amish but for now she could pamper herself.

"Woo, boy, Luke Troyer, watch out. She's setting the trap and loading it with bait." Grace whistled and clapped when she saw Leah emerge from the fitting room in the dress.

"Oh, hush, Grace, now you're talking silly." But Leah couldn't help but flush as she looked at her image in the mirror. She'd seldom seen her entire reflection from head to toe. To look at herself in clothing that definitely felt scanty and foreign yet at the same time made her feel feminine and pretty was a conflict of emotions. If you didn't know her, you might never guess she was Amish in these clothes.

"Okay, we are ready to party this Friday. Still going to pick me up?" Grace asked.

"Of course. It will probably be about 6:00."

"Sounds like a plan."

FOR THE NEXT couple days Leah tried to keep her mind on business, but it was hard. Her thoughts kept drifting to Friday night and seeing Lucas. She knew she'd be disappointed if he didn't show up. Well, time would tell, she reminded herself. Her life was in *Gott's* hands. What was meant to be was meant to be…and she couldn't help hoping this was meant to be.

FRIDAY MORNING LEAH rolled out of bed and dressed in a hurry. Now that the big day was finally here she wanted it to fly by. She couldn't wait to go to the party. She was so excited she barely swallowed a bite of the ham, eggs, and biscuits *Maemm* had waiting when Leah came downstairs dressed in her traditional Amish clothing.

By the time she'd finished washing the breakfast dishes and swept the kitchen floor *Daett* had Hershey hitched to the buggy ready to go.

"Have a *gut* day, *dochtah*," he said as he helped her into the buggy. "Go with *Gott*. Oh, and remember, your mother and I are going to visit the Kaufmanns this evening. We will not be home until late."

She assured him she'd be fine, cracked the reigns over Hershey's back and headed down the drive while *Daett* turned towards the barn.

The morning air was crisp and sweet and the birds sang *Gott's* praises loud and clear. Leah herself was singing as she guided the buggy over the crest of the hill and headed down the drive towards the road.

That's when she noticed the olive green car parked in front of their drive. Odd, the driver had completely blocked the opening to the road. Leah drew back on the reigns, moving cautiously as she approached the motionless vehicle, almost coming to a stop as she studied the nondescript sedan.

She squinted her eyes and could make out a single person behind the steering wheel. It was a male with a baseball cap pulled low over his eyes and he was staring right at her.

Leah pulled Hershey to a stop and waited. Why was that man just setting there ogling her? An uneasy feeling rippled down her spine.

Just when she was ready to turn the horse around and go get her farther the car lurched into motion, tires squealing against the pavement as the driver slammed his foot on the accelerator.

After a moment frozen in fear she managed to regain her composure. Englishers. Tourists. They were always super curious about the Amish. This was probably just another outsider who took pleasure in treating the Amish like freaks. It wasn't the first one she'd encountered.

Well, no time to think about the ways of worldly people. Time to get to work and then get ready to go to the party…and hope Luke would be there.

CHAPTER 5 - A TASTE OF ENGLISH

The weather Friday evening couldn't have been more perfect. During the day the sun shone nonstop and the temperatures were comfortably in the mid-seventies. By the time Leah picked Grace up at her house that evening the sunset painted the horizon and the insect orchestra was tuning up to perform their nightly symphony.

Like Leah, Grace was still dressed in Amish style. They would change in Cassie Walker's room once they arrived at the party. Cassie and her twin brother Clay were celebrating their 18. birthday and their parents were hosting a big get-together to mark the occasion. Although the family wasn't Amish, the Walkers were devout Christians so Leah felt at ease going to their home. It should be good fun without going too far out of her comfort zone.

The two girls arrived a bit early so they would have time to change. Cassie took them to her room and helped them transform themselves. Grace's skinny jeans, as she called them, hugged her long legs and the red sweater exposed more skin than either girl was used to. Her dark, almost black hair contrasted beautifully against the rosy top. Cassie did their makeup, providing lipstick that matched the red sweater. Grace even donned a pair of black leather high heels. All three girls burst out laughing as Grace tried to get used to walking in them.

Then it was Leah's turn to change into a modern girl. She brushed her silky hair until it gleamed and let it stream freely down her back. Carrie did her magic and Leah gawked at herself in the mirror. The soft lavender shadow and dark mascara made her eyes appear huge and just a hint of blush highlighted her cheekbones, pink gloss tinting her lips. Her legs were bared for all to see. Leah knew it was sinful to take pride in her looks but she couldn't help but admire the woman she saw in the reflection. It made her feel like a homely caterpillar breaking out of its cocoon and discovering it was a butterfly.

Guests were arriving as the three girls stepped out to the backyard where Mr. Walker had started a fire in the fire pit. Leah greeted friends and sipped a Coke as she looked around at the people gathering. No sign of Luke yet.

"Hey, let's roast hot dogs," Carrie suggested, handing them each a sharpened stick. "I want mine black as night."

Leah took her speared wiener and let the flames work their magic. In just a few minutes they were feasting on smoky hot dogs, baked beans, chips, and dip. Guests kept arriving and soon there were a few dozen people stuffing themselves full of goodies. Someone turned on the sound system and popular tunes mingled with the laughter and chatter.

Leah was having a great time but she couldn't stop her eyes from searching for Luke. He still hadn't arrived by the time Cassie and Clay were called up to the picnic table and each presented with a huge birthday cake with 18 candles flickering on top. Maybe he wasn't coming.

Leah excused herself to go back in the house and use the restroom, disappointment gnawing at her belly.

Don't be silly. She silently scolded herself as she walked through the halls. *He only said he'd come if he got his work done on time. Something must have come up.*

The first thing she saw when she returned to the back yard was Grace sitting close to Joe Kemp, an Amish boy they had known all their lives. Something looked different tonight, though. She watched as Grace laughed then rested her head on Joe's shoulder and he reached for her hand. Mmm, this was a new development.

"Leah." She whirled to see Luke standing directly behind her. Her heart accelerated at the sight of him. He looked good, strong. He, too, was dressed in English clothes. Just looking at him you could tell he did hard physical labor all day. A long sleeved red Henley style shirt hugged broad shoulders and rock hard biceps. Soft jeans rode low on his hips and outlined muscular thighs.

"I'm sorry I'm so late. We got behind at work today, but the job's done now." For a moment he let his gaze run over her in her short dress, her long hair streaming down her back, a blush painting her cheeks.

"You look like a model on the cover of a magazine."

His words made her breath catch in her throat. Did he like her better this way? This was, after all, his *rumspringa*, too. He still had the option to leave the Amish community. What if he wanted an English wife?

She didn't have a chance to say anything before a group of friends surrounded them, greeting Luke and urging him to join the horseshoe game. He went with them cheerfully but stopped and turned back to Leah.

"I'll be back soon. Don't go anywhere."

Leah nodded, a smile lighting up her face. Maybe he did like her a little bit.

The yard was well lit so the men could see to play and many of the girls stood around cheering them on. Leah walked over and watched as well. She clapped and cheered each time Luke made a ringer.

After the game was finished Luke came straight to her side.

"Let's go find something to drink and a quiet place to talk," he suggested.

They each grabbed a coke and found an unoccupied bench beneath a tree in the back corner of the yard. Here the music and chatter sounded farther away and it almost felt like they were alone.

They sat there without speaking for a while, but it was a companionable silence. Leah tipped her head back and gazed at the stars overhead. A harvest moon rose in the east, a luminescent globe almost the color of orange sherbet.

"The heavens are telling of the glory of God; And their expanse is declaring the work of His hands." Leah murmured the words as she drank in the beauty of the night.

"Psalm 19." Luke glanced up for a moment then turned his gaze back to her. "*Gott* has blessed us with many wonders, Leah. I think maybe you are one of them."

CHAPTER 6 - FEARFUL JOURNEY

If Leah was a cat she'd be purring right then. Just being with Luke felt right and hearing him say such sweet words made a warmth bubble through her veins. She didn't speak but smiled and blushed, her fingers drifting over to lightly touch his hand.

"May I speak to your parents about courting you, Leah?" She loved the old-fashioned way he made the request, an earnest plea in his eyes.

"I think that would be fine, Luke. Just fine."

"Then I'll do it after church on Sunday. Now, I wouldn't mind seeing if there's any birthday cake left. Care to join me?"

THIRTY MINUTES later the fire was dying down and the music had become softer, slower. Leah saw several couples dancing close together on the wooden deck and noticed Grace and Joe were amongst them. Amish didn't dance, but, Leah reminded herself, anything's possible in *rumspringa*. She soon found herself swaying to the soulful rhythm of the ballad playing on the stereo.

"What do you say we give this a try?"

Leah nodded and moved rather awkwardly into Luke's arms, one hand resting on his shoulder, the other clasped in his hand. It was much bigger than hers, she noticed.

This was a new experience for both of them so they simply swayed together for a few minutes before Luke became bolder. He seemed to take to dancing naturally and Leah soon found herself matching his steps. For a moment it felt as if they were all alone there, the soft night air tickling her hair against the hand he pressed along the small of her back. She knew then that if dancing was sinful she could easily learn to commit this sin on a regular basis.

When the music stopped Leah came back to reality and realized Grace and Joe were standing there, Grace chattering away. She managed to focus on her friend just in time to hear her ask a question.

"So, Joe's going to give me a ride home in his buggy. Is that okay with you, Leah? Will you be all right alone?"

"Of course. I'll be fine."

"Don't worry. I'll follow her nearly all the way there. She only has a mile or so to go after we get to my place." Luke was quick to reassure Grace.

"Okay. Well, I'm going to change and get ready to go then."

"I'm ready to change and go, too." Leah said. "I've got work in the morning."

The two girls took little time getting back into their plain clothes, laughing as they transformed back into proper young Amish ladies. They giggled and talked, Grace full of new discoveries about Joe.

"Luke's going to ask my parents about us going out." Leah confessed with a blush on her cheeks.

"Well, now, are things getting serious?"

"I don't know yet, Grace." Leah paused then gave a coy grin. "But I'm going to enjoy finding out."

AFTER ALL THE thanks were given and goodbyes were said the partygoers headed out, the English in their cars, the Amish in their buggies. Grace and Joe got away first because Luke and Leah lingered to talk to Mr. Walker about a sick neighbor who needed a wheelchair ramp built. By the time they got on the road most others were out of sight.

Hershey set a brisk pace, happy to be heading for home and the barn. Leah, too, was happy and couldn't help thinking about the events of the evening. They both thrilled and frightened her. Finding the right mate was one of the most important quests she would ever complete.

Somewhere, deep inside, this felt right. Her instinct whispered to her that Luke was the man *Gott* planned for her to be with, to bond with for life. The man who would be the head of her household, the father of her children and giver of the grandchildren Ruth and Amos Miller so hungrily desired.

But there was still a niggling doubt there. She didn't have a lot of faith in her instinct. She had sometimes acted impulsively in the past only to end up regretting her decision later.

What she did have plenty of, though, was faith in *Gott*. She trusted him to guide her through her future and lead her to the man she was destined to marry.

Leah couldn't help but smile as she heard an inner voice whisper, "And that man just might be in the buggy right behind you."

Hershey brought her rolling to a stop just as they passed Luke's driveway. She heard his voice speak to his horse Thunder then his footsteps coming up beside her.

"Would you like me to follow the rest of the way, Leah? I'd be happy to do it."

"That's not necessary, Luke. I know you're tired. It's just a short way and the weather is perfect. I'll be fine."

"If you're sure then I'll see you at church this Sunday. Good night, Leah. Thanks for making memories with me."

Leah was still blushing when she drove away. When she was out of sight she fanned at her burning cheeks. Woo, that man did arouse emotions in her she'd never felt before.

Leah drifted into daydreaming mode as the horse instinctively followed the road towards home, visions of little curly haired boys and girls with Luke's dimples dancing in her mind. It wasn't until the sharp blast of a horn ripped through the night that she realized there was a car behind her.

She and Hershey both startled at the unexpected noise. Leah gripped the reins tighter and spoke in a gentling tone to Hershey, guiding him carefully as far to the side as she could without getting too close to the deep ravine lining the edge of the road.

She expected the car to pass but instead it just kept creeping along behind her. The driver would occasionally rev the engine, sounding like a roaring lion at her tail. Headlights beamed through the small isinglass window at the back of the buggy. The car was close behind her…too close. She slowed even further. Surely he would pass her any moment.

The engine revved again and Leah nibbled at her lip. The hair on her arms stood up and a shiver of apprehension tickled her spine. Why was this guy doing this? Was he trying to scare the wits out of her? If so, it was working.

Okay, slowing down wasn't improving the situation. She cracked the reins over Hershey's back and urged the horse to pick up speed. They only had a little ways to go before they reached the driveway to the farm.

Hershey's hooves pounded over the pavement as loud and fast as Leah's heart pounded in her chest. She barely slowed the horse down when he took the corner into the lane.

A few yards up Leah turned in her seat to see if the car followed her into the drive but the vehicle slowly crept on past, giving a final blast of its horn.

Leah's breath caught in her chest.

It was the same green car that'd been at the end of the drive this morning.

CHAPTER 7 - THE TALK

Leah was still shaking by the time she had Hershey stabled and let herself into the dark house. The big old farmhouse was filled with silence and she remembered her parents were out for the evening.

She moved to look out the window, searching for any clue that someone was out there. A small scream broke from her throat when the bushes parted and a shadowy figure stepped onto the lawn. Her hand clutched at her throat, her eyes straining to make out who was there. Her shoulders sagged with relief when she realized it was just a deer heading towards the creek down the hill.

She was home. She was safe. Leah kept reminding herself of those two facts as she headed up to her bedroom. But the incident had left her shaken. She changed into a long cotton nightgown and curled up in bed to read the Bible for a while. As usual the beautiful words of the Scriptures soothed her and calmed her fears.

She heard her parents come home a short while later and was soon lulled to sleep by the soft murmur of their voices in their room next door.

L*EAH* K*EPT* a sharp lookout as she drove to work the next morning but didn't catch a glimpse of a green car nearby. She breathed a sigh of relief when she walked in the quilt shop and closed the door. She couldn't shake the feeling she was being watched.

The day was filled with inquisitive tourists strolling through the shop, the Saturday morning quilting class, and preparing orders to be shipped to online customers. She didn't have time to fret about possible stalkers or olive green sedans until they locked the door at closing time.

She and Sherry leaned against a counter in the back room and caught their breath. This had been one of the busiest days they'd ever had and Sherry couldn't help grinning with pleasure. The cash register had been busy today.

After a couple minutes of celebration, Leah's smile dimmed.

"Sherry, I need to ask you something. Remember that man who was asking all the questions about a Miller girl?"

"Sure, I remember. Why?"

"Have you seen him around anymore?"

"Noooo," she drew her answer out slowly, raising her eyebrows. "What's going on, Leah"

Leah hesitated. She hadn't told anyone about the strange events that had happened yesterday but she felt like she needed to talk about it. She trusted Sherry would hold her confidence and began telling her everything. Sherry's eyes grew wide when she detailed the car following her last night."

"Leah, you need to tell your parents about this...and the police, too. This could be some kind of wacko or something."

"You know the Amish don't go to the police with their problems, Sherry. And I hate to tell my parents. It would only worry them."

"But they could help keep an eye on you. I don't think you should be riding around alone right now. I just don't like it."

Leah didn't want to admit she was a little concerned herself but she trusted *Gott* to protect her and keep her safe. She wasn't going to let fear rule her life. She'd keep alert, be vigilant, and pray.

But she was glad that she had told someone about the weird occurrences. Listening to herself talk about them made them feel less threatening, more like pranks. The last two events may not even be connected to the man asking questions.

"Don't worry about it, please, Sherry. It's probably nothing. Besides, *Gott* is the only protector I need."

"You're right, Leah, you're right. But remember this: God helps those that help themselves. So why don't I pick you up a cell phone so you'll have a way to call for help if you need it."

Leah tilted her head and thought for a minute. It would probably be okay temporarily, at least while she was in rumspringa."

"That might be a good idea. But I only need one of those prepaid phones without any long term contracts. And of course I insist on paying for it myself."

"We'll worry about that later. Now wait here and I'll have a phone for you in no time." Sherry pulled her in for a hug. "And please, please, Leah, be careful."

"I promise." Leah returned the hug. "And you promise not to worry about me. *Gott's* got this covered."

TRUE TO HER word Sherry brought the phone, charged it, and helped Leah activate. Leah made a couple test calls then stuck the phone in her simple drawstring bag. She had to admit it did make her feel safer knowing it was there and she had a way to call for help if needed.

She spent that evening washing her hair and readying her garments for church the next day. Thinking about it made butterflies flutter in her stomach. Luke was going to talk to her parents tomorrow about coming to call on her. She knew they'd agree but Amish tradition demanded that they all talk it over before the young couple started dating. The idea still made her nervous.

SUNDAY MORNING DAWNED sunny and cool, a hint of autumn filling the air. Leah dressed in a burgundy dress and a navy blue apron before adding her white *kapp*. Once downstairs she helped Maemm pack up their contributions to the dinner that would be served after the service. They were taking potato salad, deviled eggs, home canned pickles, and zucchini bread. Leah found herself humming as she loaded the goodies into the buggy.

Church was held at the Hochstetler's home that day and attendance was good. The sermon seemed extra-long to Leah that morning as her nerves began to tense. She cast several glances from under lowered eyelashes at Luke and caught him staring at her once. Was he as nervous as she was?

Finally the service concluded and dinner was served. Leah helped keep food coming to the tables, almost too anxious to eat anything herself. What if Luke had changed his mind? What if he'd decided not to court her after all?

Shortly after the last of the food had been put away and people were still mingling, talking and laughing with each other, Leah saw Luke striding over to where she sat with her parents, a determined look on his face.

"*Gut* afternoon, Miller family. The Lord has blessed us with another beautiful day." Leah waited nervously as Luke and her parents exchanged small talk for a bit, discussing the shed Luke was going to build for her *daett* and his family's health until Leah was about to burst with anxiety. How could he be so calm?

Then he uttered the words she'd been waiting to hear.

"I was wondering if the four of us could find somewhere quiet to talk in private."

CHAPTER 8 - SHOTS IN THE DARK

As soon as Luke uttered the words Leah saw a happy smile cross her mother's face. She knew what was coming. Her father probably did, too, but he took his role seriously and led them to a quiet corner of the big porch that wrapped around the old farmhouse.

Now that it was over Leah laughed at herself for being so nervous. The conversation had gone well and now, much to her delight, Luke would be driving her home from this evening's singing. Singings were traditional, restricted to young singles of courting age. It was kind of the Amish answer to teen dances where young people could get to know one another. They were always held on the same Sundays as church, every other Sunday. Leah had always attended alone or with girlfriends before. Tonight would be different.

Although Amish didn't play musical instruments, the songs the young people enjoyed in the evening were usually less somber than those sang in church. Tonight the blend of youthful voices sounded especially beautiful to Leah's ears.

Grace was there with Joe sticking close to her side. The two girls managed to squeeze in a few minutes alone together and share a little girl talk. When Leah questioned her about how she was feeling now about remaining Amish Grace blushed and cast a look at Joe.

"Maybe I don't have to go searching for happiness elsewhere. We'll see what *Gott's* plan is for me. And what about you? Has Luke had "the talk" with your parents yet?"

Leah blushed and nodded. "This afternoon."

"So he's driving you home tonight? Well, you go, girl." Leah couldn't help but laugh. Grace always managed to make her smile.

WHEN THE FESTIVITIES drew to a close Luke helped Leah into his open carriage. Thunder took off headed towards home. Conversation came easy to them as they rolled along, talking of news of friends, Luke telling her about a letter he'd received from his mother back in Pennsylvania. Leah was super aware of Luke's brawny body next to hers, enjoying his warmth.

She was surprised to realize they were already nearing her home. It was just about a quarter mile past the next intersection. She knew Luke would stay awhile and they would set in the living room and talk. She could serve him some of the chocolate fudge brownies she had made last night. If they were lucky there would be some fresh whipped cream to go on top.

THE GUNSHOT CAME out of nowhere. The blast shattered the night at the same time Leah felt the bullet whiz past her face. Before she had time to even scream, a second shot rang out, this time creasing Thunder's flank. The horse shrieked with pain and reared, his front hooves flailing the air.

Everything seemed to happen too quickly to comprehend after that. Thunder came down off balance and lurched into the ravine, taking the buggy with him. The wheels bounced over boulders and logs, then tipped on its side. Leah felt herself fly through the air then landed, hard, belly down on the ground, her face scratched and whipped by the thick foliage filling the gully. Shock kept her from feeling any pain that moment, though. Her only thought was for Luke.

Fighting to catch the breath that had been knocked out of her, she began to claw her way up the overgrown hillside, her eyes searching the dark gully for any sign of Luke. She had just managed to get her head level with the road when she heard the roar of an engine and caught sight of a car flying down the road. She couldn't be sure in the dark, but it looked like a sedan.

An olive green sedan.

No time to worry about that now. She had to find Luke. There. Down the ravine on the other side of the buggy. He lay still and motionless.

Leah prayed as hard as she ever had in her life as she stumbled towards the prone figure and hunted for a pulse. Yes! He was alive. Blood ran down his face from a deep cut on his head and his arm was twisted at a strange angle.

She had to have help and she had to have it now. She glanced frantically around, praying to see approaching headlights. She didn't want to leave Luke alone long enough to run to her parent's house for help.

Then she remembered. The cell phone; she had to find her purse, hope the cell phone had survived the crash, and call for help.

Once again she began to scour the ground and luck was with her. She spotted her bag and snatched it up. The phone was intact. She whispered a prayer of thanks and dialed 911.

Then she hurried back to Luke's side, knelt in the weeds, and prayed.

CHAPTER 9 - ATTACKED!

By the time the ambulance arrived Luke was regaining consciousness. Moaning, he tried to sit up but Leah pushed him back to the ground.

"Stay still, Luke. Help's here. Just don't move until they look at you."

"Are...you okay?" His voice was weak, his gaze raking over her. "Your face...you're bleeding."

"I'm fine. Just a couple scratches."

"Th...Thunder?"

"I think he's going to be okay. There's a vet on his way to see to him."

A few seconds later they were surrounded by EMTs, police officers, and neighbors who had come to see what the ruckus was about, including Leah's parents. Luke was loaded into the ambulance and it took off for the hospital.

Leah answered everyone's questions the best she could but it had all happened so fast she didn't remember many details. Sheriff Weeks was patient with her, patting her arm and reassuring that it wasn't unusual to have foggy memories of such a traumatic event.

"Well, it was probably just some poacher deer hunting out of season anyway. We'll do our best to find out who it was." He reached in his pocket and pulled out a business card." If you remember anything else get a hold of me."

Leah took the card and dropped it in her purse. Should she tell him about the other incidents? No, it would go against the *Ordnung* to involve the police in their private business if it could be avoided.

Leah's parents led her to back to the house, supportive arms around her. She had refused medical attention at the scene. She only had some scratches on her face and a few dozen bruises across her body. She'd be fine.

She sat in a kitchen chair while *Maemm* cleaned the abrasions. This was certainly not the way she thought this evening would come to an end. She closed her eyes and whispered a prayer for Luke.

THE NEXT MORNING Leah walked to the phone box at the end of the drive and called the hospital. She ached all over and wasn't going to work today, but her conscience felt better going to use the phone at the end of the drive instead of using the cell phone for other than true emergencies.

The operator connected her to Luke's room and she felt her heart lift when she heard how well he sounded.

"I've got 18 stitches in my forehead from a rock I hit, a slight concussion, and a broken left arm, but it could have been much worse. I'm a lucky man, thank *Gott*. They say I'll probably be discharged this afternoon."

"I'm so glad you're not hurt worse." Leah whispered a prayer of thanksgiving. "Do you need a ride home when you get discharged?

"No, my nephew is coming to get me. But I would like to see you this evening. May I come over after dinner?"

"Are you sure you feel up to it?"

"I feel fine. I just want to see you with my own eyes to be sure you're okay."

His sweet words melted Leah's heart.

"I want to see you, too," she whispered. "Goodbye until tonight, then."

Since Leah didn't go to work that day she spent the time doing quiet chores like sewing on buttons, mending socks, and catching up on correspondence with friends in other Amish communities.

Maemm fussed around her all afternoon, making sure she had everything nearby. Leah had to admit she ached all over, the scratches fiery red across her face, aches reverberating in muscles she never realized she had but her mother's hovering was starting to get on her nerves.

"Aren't you and Daett going to the Fritz's for the anniversary dinner?" *Maemm* had been looking forward to the get-together for quite a while.

"Oh, we've decided to stay home with you."

"That isn't necessary, *Maemm*. I'm fine. Please, I will feel terrible if you miss the party because of me. Go."

"But you might need something." *Maemm* was still shaking her head negatively.

"And if I do, I can get it myself. Please, *Maemm*, go and have fun."

"Well, I suppose we could go for a little while."

Two hours later Leah stood on the porch and waved to her parents as they rolled down the drive. She turned back inside and went to the kitchen to eat a chicken salad sandwich and some canned peaches for her dinner.

Despite the headache building behind her eyes, she felt excitement blooming as it came time for Luke's arrival. Since her parents weren't home they would sit on the porch in plain sight of any passing traffic.

She finished up the few dishes she had used then decided to walk the letters she had written today to the mailbox at the bottom of the drive. Maybe some fresh air would help to relieve the headache. She wrapped a shawl around her shoulders and grabbed the letters then headed down the lane.

It was a chilly evening but still lovely. A gentle breeze tickled her dress against her legs and brought some color to her cheeks. Their border collie Lady chose to take a break from her puppies and accompanied Leah on her walk.

She had just put the letters in the box and raised the flag to alert the mailman when she heard a rustling behind her. She whirled and saw a man emerge from the cornfield right in front of her.

She stood frozen for a moment, shock rooting her feet to the ground but when the scarecrow looking man lunged at her, she screamed and turned to dart away.

She wasn't fast enough. He grabbed her by her cape and hauled her hard against his long lean body. She was so close she could smell the stale cigarette smoke on his breath.

"Let me go, let me go," she screamed and twisted, trying to escape his steely grip.

"Sorry, lady. I've got a job to do. Now you gotta die."

His words renewed her strength and she managed to pull one arm free and screamed again, her fear and rage erupting in a howl. Lady launched herself forward and sank her teeth into the man's thigh. The man yelped and smacked Lady with the fist. The dog let out a cry and fell to the ground unconscious.

Leah took advantage of the distraction and jerked free from the man's grip. She'd have to go past him to get back to the drive so instead she began to run through the cornfield, slapping stalks out of her way. Her breath came in long, scraping gasps as she pushed deeper into the dense field.

Her shawl fell off her shoulders and she kept going, adrenalin making her legs pump like pistons. If she could just lose him in the maize of towering stalks she might have a chance.

Hope ran out when she felt the man tackle her to the ground. She tasted dirt as her face hit the soil and her breath whooshed out of her chest as he landed on top of her.

The words of the 23. Psalm began racing through her mind. *Yeah, though I walk through the valley of the shadow of death I shall fear no evil.*

She thought at first it was *Gott* she heard calling her name, but it wasn't. It was Luke. She heard him flailing through the field, felt the man's weight lift off her as he rose up to confront the fast approaching Luke. The moment she was free she leapt to her feet and turned to see Luke bursting into sight.

And then she saw the gun in the man's hands. He raised it and aimed directly at Luke's chest.

"Noooo," she screamed as she launched herself onto the man's back, knocking him off balance. A single shot echoed into the night.

At the same moment Luke barreled into the man and brought his cast encrusted left arm crashing down onto the man's temple. The man crumpled like a discarded potato chip bag.

Moments later Luke prodded the man towards the driveway, his hands tied securely behind his back with Leah's apron strings. Lady, now conscious, met them as they came out of the cornfield, growled menacingly and bared her teeth at the stranger who had attacked her and her mistress. Only Luke's calming words kept her from ripping into the evil man.

CHAPTER 10 - EPILOGUE

It was over. The sheriff came and took custody of the attacker. Leah and Luke didn't feel bad about calling in the law this time. The man was an Englisher. Let the outside world take care of their lawbreakers themselves.

But Leah hadn't forgotten about those words he'd spoken. "I've got a job to do. Now you gotta die." Why was he supposed to kill her?

The answers came the next day when Sherriff Weeks came to call. Luke was there as well, the Sheriff having picked him up on his way to the Millers. When Leah saw the two of them at the door, their expressions grim, her gut tightened up. The news didn't look good.

"Leah, run get your father from the fields. Gentleman, please come in. May I get you some tea and cookies?

Leah didn't have far to go. Her father had seen the brown and tan sheriff's car pull into the drive and was on his way. Together they returned to the house and joined the others sitting at the kitchen table, anxious to hear what the sheriff had to say.

"The man we took into custody last night is named Virgil Shoemaker. He says he was hired to kill you, Leah." The granite faced man looked directly at her as he rubbed his jaw. "In fact, he says you're not Leah Miller at all. Says your name should be Tiffany Ashbury."

"Why, that's crazy talk. I'm Leah Miller, always have been. Where did he get such a ridiculous idea?" Leah turned startled eyes towards her parents, expecting them to reinforce her fervent words. Instead, Ruth Miller's face had taken on a ghostly hue and Amos bowed his head, his hands clenched on the table before him.

"He's wrong, isn't he? *Maemm*? *Daett*?" A frantic edge came into her voice and she leapt to her feet as she watched her parents' unexpected reactions. "What's he talking about?"

Ruth Miller choked back a sob. "I knew we should have told her the truth long ago, Amos. I knew it."

Luke stood and moved to stand protectively at Leah's side.

Amos Miller shook his gray head sadly. "Leah, we have sinned. We didn't want anyone to ever know our secret."

"I don't understand. What are you talking about?

"*Dochtah*, you are not our natural born child." He looked up, a sheen of tears in his faded brown eyes. "We found you on our doorstep."

"Oh, Leah, you were such a beautiful baby, laid right there on our steps like a gift from *Gott*. We prayed long and hard for a child and then, there you were." Ruth brought her apron up to wipe her eyes. "I'd had so many miscarriages, lost so many babies, it seemed like a miracle that you were given to us. We lied to everyone and told them I had concealed my pregnancy for fear it would again not come to term. We said I had a home birth and filed for a birth certificate."

The words knocked her knees out from under her and she collapsed back onto the chair. Luke's hand grasped her shoulder, helping to keep her from shattering with shock.

Sheriff Weeks cleared his throat before continuing. "It didn't take long for Shoemaker to start singing like a bird. He gave us the name of the man who hired him. A fellow named Grayson Ashbury. We picked him up this morning. He says he's your half-brother, Leah."

Another shock that slapped her across the face. She had a brother.

Then she remembered. That brother wanted her dead.

"I don't understand any of this."

"Well, to make a long story short, this guy is the son of George Ashbury and Annamarie Grayson Ashbury, head honchos at Grayson Pharmaceuticals in Chicago. Technically, the wife inherited the company and had all the control. Her husband was just a figurehead. He had an affair and got a girl pregnant."

"My…my mother?" The words sounded strange to her ears. Ruth Miller was the only mother she'd ever known.

"Yes. Ashbury knew if his wife found out he'd be out without a penny so he paid the girl to get rid of you. But she didn't. She used the money to come here and stay with a friend until you were born. By then she'd done her research and picked out the Millers to be your parents." The sheriff stopped talking long enough to take a long drink of his tea.

"Then the wife died a couple years ago and the husband came into all the money. Turns out he wasn't going to have long to enjoy it, though. Seems your, um, mother eventually told Ashbury about you and told him you'd been growing up Amish, as far from his world as she could get you."

Amos Miller couldn't contain his anger, jumping to his feet. "So he decided to kill her?"

"No, no, Mr. Miller. Just the opposite. He wanted to find her so he could put her in his will. You see, he'd been diagnosed with terminal cancer and didn't want to die with Leah here on his conscious. That's why he hired a private detective to find her."

The man with all the questions, Leah thought.

"But by the time the detective was pretty sure he'd located you old man Ashbury was in bad shape and his son was handling all his affairs. Apparently junior didn't take the news well that he would be expected to split the family wealth with you. That's where Shoemaker comes in."

"Well, thank *Gott* he wasn't a very skilled hitman" Luke squeezed her shoulder tighter. Leah felt comforted by the warmth of his hand but icy shivers still tickled her spine.

"No, Shoemaker wasn't a professional killer, just some guy that was in way too deep to Grayson Ashbury. He used to work for the company as an accountant and Grayson caught him skimming money from the company's accounts to his own. So he was given a choice. Prison and disgrace or kill you."

Leah was numb. None of this seemed real.

"One more thing, Leah." The sheriff eyed her speculatively. "The senior Ashbury did have his will changed before he died. Since he wasn't sure of your name he had it stated that anyone that could prove his paternity would be an equal heir. If the DNA test pans out, that makes you a multimillionaire."

"Dear Gott." Ruth Miller moaned. "Leah, can you ever forgive us? We put your life in danger and all we ever wanted to do was protect you, to keep you from harm and raise you up as a child of Christ." She buried her face in her hands, silent sobs racking her body.

The kitchen spun around as Leah attempted to grasp everything being pushed at her. Her entire life was a lie. Everything she though she knew about herself was untrue. For a moment she felt like she couldn't breathe and rose from the table and dashed for the door.

"I need some air," was all she could gasp as she dashed outside, the screen door slamming behind her.

And then she started running. She didn't know where she was going. She just ran. Finally when she reached the creek at the bottom of the hill she stopped and collapsed onto a fallen log and let the thoughts churn through her head, tears running down her face. All she knew to do know was pray for guidance.

She didn't know how long she'd been sitting there when Luke came up behind her and softly called her name.

She turned a pale face towards him and gave him a bit of a smile.

"Mind if I join you?"

"Please do." She patted the space next to her on the log and he sat, stretching his long legs out before him.

"Well, that was a whole lot to take in, wasn't it?" He reached out and wiped a tear from her cheek with the ball of his thumb. "Here, take this."

He held out a handkerchief and she took it and blotted at her wet face.

"You could say that. I mean, I just discovered that nothing about me is real, I'm not even who I thought I was."

"But that is where you're wrong, Leah. You are still who you have always been, the *dochtah* of *Gott*, a woman of faith and principles. None of that has changed. Just now you have some decisions to face."

"I've been sitting here praying to understand all these new facts." Leah drew a deep breath. "I keep hearing one Bible verse from Psalms repeating through my head. *I will instruct you and teach you in the way you should go; I will counsel you with my eye upon you.* And he has, Luke. He's been teaching me all my life. I love my life just the way it is. I love being Leah Miller. I don't want to be anyone else. I have everything I need, including the best parents a girl could hope for. I don't want that money."

"Then give it away to those who need it. And don't change. Stay true to yourself. If you are happy and can be at peace with that decision, than that is what you should do. But think long and hard, Leah. This is the chance of a lifetime. You could live in luxury. You would never have to work, never have to scrimp and save. Are you very sure you want to give that up?"

Leah looked deep into Luke's honey brown eyes and smiled. "I've never been surer of anything in my life."

"So you are happy being Leah Miller." Luke reached out and took her hand in his. "Tell me, do you think you could be happy being Leah Troyer, plain Amish wife?"

"Blissfully." She felt tears spring to her eyes again but this time they were tears of happiness. "I can't think of anything that would make me happier."

Luke raised his hands to his lips and kissed them softly. "Shall we go talk to your parents? They're worried sick you will leave them or hate them for their deceit."

"I could never do that. Yes, let's go back to the house." Luke rose and held her hand as they strolled up the path together. Leah couldn't wait to see her parents, to wipe away their worries, to tell them of her love for them.

And maybe, one day soon, she would give her parents the only gift they'd ever asked her for: grandchildren. She turned to look at Luke and found him smiling at her. Here they were, him with a cast on his arm and a bandage on his forehead, her with scratches across her face, battered and wounded. But to Leah, the love they shared made them beautiful together.

Amish Investigation

THE MYSTERIOUS DISAPEARANCE

CHAPTER 1

"Ouch," Justine exclaimed as the sharp needle pierced her fingertip. She examined the end of her finger and put it to her mouth, lightly sucking the small wound. She didn't want the blood on the rug she was making or on her clothes. Her clothes might not be expensive, but they were hard work to make and hard work to wash out by hand.

"What happened?" asked Amity, Justine's best friend who sat beside her working on her own rug. "You never prick yourself."

"I know," Justine sighed as she removed her finger from her mouth and looked at it again. The bleeding seemed to have stopped and she could barely even see the mark the needle had left. "My mind wasn't really on it, that's all."

"Is something wrong?" Amity asked, a note of concern in her voice.

"Everything," Justine wanted to say but didn't.

She gave a half shrug. "Nothing really, I was just thinking about something. It's not important."

Justine went back to her rug making, careful this time not to hurt herself again. With a great effort, she concentrated on the rug and the needle, trying to push out the other thoughts that kept trying to creep back in. If she could just find her rhythm with the rug making, she could concentrate on that, but she was having so much trouble focussing, she couldn't get the rhythm.

"It obviously is important," Amity said watching her for a moment before resuming her rug making. "Come on, what's going on? Is it Mark?"

"Sort of," Justine said. She didn't really want to talk about it but she knew Amity would get it out of her. Last time she had talked about it, it had been to Mark and that hadn't ended well.

"Justine, spill," Amity said. It was more of a demand than a request.

Justine knew there was little point in arguing. Amity would badger her until she gave in and told her. She decided to do it the easy way and just tell her.

"I spoke to Mark a couple of days ago about what happened with Anna. He didn't like what I had to say and he practically ordered me to let it go."

"She is his sister Justine. Maybe he's still upset that she left and he doesn't want to talk about it."

"It's not that," Justine said. She was going to have to tell Amity everything, because what she was saying now wasn't making much sense.

With a sigh she put down the partially made rug and continued. "I don't think Anna left here Amity. I think something has happened to her. And I believe their father is covering it up."

"And you told Mark that?"

"Yes," Justine said nodding her head. "I thought he had a right to know. If it was me, I would want to know. Wouldn't you?"

Amity ignored her question and asked one of her own. "What made you even think such a thing?"

"Anna really believed in this life. She loved it here. We talked about it after Mark and I got engaged. She said she could never imagine a different life, and she couldn't understand why anyone would choose to leave here."

"Maybe she changed her mind. People change."

"I know that, but it just doesn't fit with the happy girl I knew. Maybe I'm wrong, I'm not certain of course, but Mark became so defensive when I mentioned it to him that it made me think he suspected something similar and didn't want to admit it."

"Or maybe he was just annoyed because you accused his father of something so immoral. Or maybe he was upset because his sister left. There could be many explanations for it touching a nerve with him."

"I don't think her father hurt her or anything. I think he's knows what happened and he's either covering it up to save Mark's feelings, or to save the family's reputation. But if something has happened to her, Mark has a right to know."

"Did you make it clear to Mark that weren't accusing his father of something terrible?"

"I think so." Justine said. She looked down into her lap as she said it. Maybe she hadn't made it clear enough.

"You think so? You should talk to him, make sure he knows for definite."

"That's just the thing though, he's made it quite clear we won't be discussing it any further."

Amity looked at Justine, her eyebrows raised.

"Oh no, nothing like that," Justine said quickly, seeing that her friend thought Mark had been violent with her. "He just got so upset and said he would rather I didn't bring it up again. Now I can't decide what to do for the best. Do I mention it and risk upsetting him again when it could be for nothing, or do I keep quiet about it knowing that maybe Anna's in trouble and needs our help?"

"I wish I could help you, but I really don't know what I would do in that situation," Amity said. "Have you prayed on it."

Justine nodded. "I have. I believe God would want me to make sure Anna's definitely ok, but what would I know about God's will. I don't profess to be important enough to be a part of His plan."

"We're all part of His plan Justine. You have to do what you think is right."

"I know," Justine sighed, "but it's hard. What if I lose Mark?"

"You won't lose him," Amity said. "He loves you. And even if you do, maybe that's the way things had to be."

Justine didn't like the thought of that, but she feared Amity was right.

"The only thing I can think of doing is asking around a bit. Talking to Anna's friends. I need to see if I can find anything out that will convince me one way or the other of whether she left or whether she's in danger. Then I will act on it, whichever way it goes."

"That's still not without risk," Amity said. "Mark might find out you've been asking questions."

"I know," Justine said, "but it's the only thing I can think of to do, and I have to do something. I'm hoping that Anna's friends will be subtle and not tell him we've spoken of her. I have to know one way or the other."

She bent down and picked her rug back up. "I just have to know, one way or the other," she repeated.

"It sounds like your mind is already made up," Amity commented.

"I guess it is," Justine said.

CHAPTER 2

Mark stood up and straightened his back with a loud crack. He wiped the back of his hand over his forehead to remove some of the sweat and grime. It was hard work repairing Eli's shed roof, but Eli was his best friend so when he had asked for Mark's help, he had agreed readily. That's what friends did, they helped each other.

"Are you looking forward to seeing Justine at the gathering tomorrow?" Eli asked Mark as he continued putting the new canvas into the hole in the roof. Once the canvas was in place, they could mix and add the bitumen. It would only be another couple of hours.

Mark shrugged. "Yes, I guess I am."

"You guess you are? What happened? Did you two have a fight or something?" Eli asked, surprised. Mark and Justine never fought.

"Sort of," said Mark. "It was more of a disagreement that a fight. You know how Anna left the village?"

"Sure," Eli nodded. "Justine isn't thinking of doing the same is she?"

"No, nothing like that," Mark said. "She came to me a couple of days ago and said that she doesn't believe that Anna would just up and leave. She said Anna always had a really strong faith and that she loved the life here too much to ever leave. She thinks Anna might be in danger, and she accused my father of lying to cover something up."

"Really?" Eli said, a concerned frown crossing his face. "It's not like Justine to make wild accusations like that. Did she say why she thought that?"

"Not really," Mark said. "I think it's just because she knew how much Anna loved her life here. She did, I'm not denying that, but people change, and sometimes, they end up wanting more. That's all that happened with Anna. I'm not really sure if Justine thinks my father hurt Anna, or what she thinks happened, but I don't like her making accusations against him. It's not right. He would never hurt Anna."

"Did you ask her exactly what she meant? I don't think she would accuse your father of hurting Anna. Maybe you misunderstood."

"Maybe I did misunderstand. I didn't ask her to clarify exactly what she meant. It just made me so mad. I think I might have jumped to the wrong conclusion. I don't know. But I pretty much told her to drop it and not talk to me about it again."

Eli winced.

"I know," Mark agreed. "It makes it sound like I know something too."

"I wasn't thinking that. Justine knows you would never harm Anna; she knows how close you two were. Maybe that's why she thinks something's wrong. She would expect Anna to have come to you with this. I just winced because I think you were perhaps a little harsh on her."

"I probably was a bit harsh," Mark agreed, "but it's done now, and I really would prefer her to not keep on bringing this up. It hurts me to know that Anna would just up and leave without saying good bye. I feel like I failed her somehow, that she felt she couldn't come to me, and Justine talking about her all the time just keeps making me think about it more. And now I've made myself unapproachable for Justine too. It's all such a mess. What if I lose her because of this?"

"You won't," Eli said forcefully. "No way. Justine loves you and she knows you love her. She'll get over it and see that what you did was for the best. It won't look good for her if she's seen to be making trouble for your father. She must know that."

"You're right. The rational part of me know you're right and that I did the right thing, although I could have been a bit gentler about it, but there's a part of me that feels guilty. Guilty that Anna left. Guilty that Justine thinks bad things about my father. And guilty that I was too harsh with her."

"You have nothing to feel guilty about. Anna is a grown woman. If she wants a different life to the one she would have here, it's up to her to decide that. You don't have to feel guilty about what Justine says or thinks. You can't control her thoughts. And I'm sure she will understand in time why you had to put a stop to this nonsense."

"So you don't think there's any chance she could be right then?"

"No," Eli said shaking his head. "No of course not. Why, do you?"

Mark paused for a second. "No. I don't. I really don't. But then Justine isn't the hysterical type. She wouldn't just jump to this conclusion for no good reason. Do you think I should talk to her?"

"Honestly, no, not about this. I think you should just let it go and hope she does the same. You can't have your fiancé going around the village casting aspersions on your father's character. It wouldn't be right. You did what you had to do, and Justine must know that."

"Yeah," Mark said, but he didn't sound convinced. He paused.

"Yeah," he said again with a nod. This time he sounded more like he believed it. He still wasn't sure he had done the right thing, but it was done now and he would have to stand by his words. He just Eli was right about Justine accepting them. He couldn't bear to lose her.

CHAPTER 3

Justine stood beside Mark, a happy smile beaming from her face. The whole village was gathered in the village square to hold a celebration to welcome the newest addition to their community.

A new baby born strong and healthy was always cause for a celebration and this one was no exception. The villagers gathered in small groups, talking and laughing. The trestle table in the centre of the square held plates of various foods, all prepared by the women of the village.

The proud parents had never looked happier as everyone congratulated them and commented on their new baby.

Justine was so happy, partly because she was caught up in the party atmosphere of the gathering, and partly because Mark seemed to be his normal self again. When they had first met up to go to the gathering together, there had been an awkward silence.

Mark had broken it by telling Justine how pretty she looked. She had smiled, and that was it. The awkwardness was over and they had gone back to the comfortable place they were always in.

And now they joined in the celebrations, cooing over the baby and talking to their friends and neighbours. Mark's father had come over and chatted briefly to them before moving on to talk to his brother and sister-in-law.

Justine had been a little ashamed that she had accused him of covering up whatever had happened to Anna. He looked so sad. He was obviously missing Anna.

A little voice in Justine's head had questioned his sadness. Was he missing her, or was his sadness born of the guilt he would feel about lying about what had happened to her?

Justine had dismissed the thought. Mark had made it clear he wanted the subject dropped, and she didn't want to start another argument, not when things were back to normal between them. She had done her part. She had voiced her concerns. What more could she do?

She knew the answer to that. She had to get more information, but the gathering wasn't the time or place for that. She just wanted to enjoy the day and put all thoughts of Anna out of her mind. She would talk to Anna's friends tomorrow she promised herself. Today was about welcoming a new baby into the world, and she wasn't going to taint that with an argument with Mark.

Justine and Mark were sat together on a blanket. They had just finished eating, as had most of the others. They laughed and chatted together, discussing their plans for the future.

Justine smiled over towards the new baby. "I want at least four," she smiled.

"Four sounds good," Mark agreed. "I can't wait to start my life with you Justine."

"Me either," Justine said. She couldn't believe she had thought she would lose him.

The baby's father stood up and moved to the centre of the gathering. He addressed the people.

"My wife and I would like to thank each and every one of you for what you have done for us today. Thank you all for contributing to make this day so special, and of course, thank you for being here and joining us in formally welcoming our son into the world. It means so much to both of us."

He sat back down to a round of applause and cheers.

"I'm just going to go and have a word with Eli," Mark said to Justine after the applause died down. "Will you be ok here for a minute?"

Justine smiled. "Of course," she said.

Justine watched Mark walk away, a smile on her face. She was so glad they were ok again. She closed her eyes and turned her face up to the sun, enjoying the warmth on her skin.

As she sat back, leaning on her hands, with her head back and her eyes closed, she felt eyes watching her and she heard feet shuffling. She opened her eyes. A girl who looked to Justine to be around sixteen stood before her. She smiled at the girl, curious as to why she was watching her.

Justine vaguely recognised the girl. She lived a block or two away from her, but she couldn't remember ever saying more than good morning to her.

"Hello," The girl said. She looked down at her feet and picked awkwardly at her sleeve. "May I sit down for a moment please?"

"Sure," Justine nodded. She pulled her feet under her making room for the girl. "What's wrong?"

"Is it that obvious?" the girl said.

Justine smiled. "Yes," she said.

The girl sat cross legged looking down into her lap.

"You think something happened to Anna don't you?" the girl said, finally looking up from her lap.

Justine wasn't sure what to say. She had no idea who this girl was or why she was here. As she tried to think of a way to answer her, the girl spoke again.

"I'm sorry, that came out all wrong. My name is Sarah. I was Anna's best friend. I think you might be right, but I don't know what to do about it. That's why I came to you."

"What makes you think I think something happened to her?"

"I overheard Mark and Eli talking about an argument you and Mark had about it," Sarah admitted, her face flushing pink with embarrassment.

"It's ok," Justine told her. "I honestly don't know what to think anymore, but it seemed very out of character for Anna to just up and leave."

Sarah nodded. "I know. There's something else. Something that makes me think something did happen, but I swore to her I wouldn't tell anyone."

Justine waited for her to go on and when she didn't, she realised she was waiting for Justine to tell her she could trust her.

"Sarah its ok. I won't tell anyone you told me. If it's important you have to tell me so I can try to help her."

Sarah paused for a second then her face set with a steely resolve. She had made her decision.

"A couple of months ago, Anna did think about leaving, but she decided against it. She said she would miss everyone too much and she would miss the life. She wasn't cut out for the big world, she wouldn't cope out there. She told me she was going to talk to her father and try to make him understand. And then she disappeared."

"What did she tell him Sarah? What did he need to understand?"

"Anna was promised to Amos. She couldn't marry him because she didn't love him. She loved Jacob. When she said she wouldn't leave, she also said nothing her father said or did could make her marry for anything except love."

Justine's eyes widened with shock. Had Anna's father hurt her rather than have her publicly disobey him? Justine didn't want to believe that, but it was starting to look more likely by the second.

CHAPTER 4

"We need to talk. Now," Mark said. He didn't raise his voice, but by his tone, Justine knew he was beyond angry.

She nodded to Sarah who stood up and practically ran away from them. Mark sat down in the space Sarah vacated.

"How long had you been there?" Justine asked quietly.

"Long enough to hear that girl accuse my father of murder and to know you did nothing to change her mind," Mark said, his voice dangerously low. "Did the conversation we had two days ago mean nothing to you? Do I mean so little to you that you would go behind my back on this?"

"It's not like that," Justine said, her voice breaking. "She came to me and said she needed to tell me something. What was I supposed to do? Send her away?"

"What were you supposed to do?" Mark asked, incredulous. "What you were supposed to do was tell that girl to mind her business. That my father is a good man. That Anna chose to leave of her own accord for reasons known only to her."

"Even if I don't believe it?" Justine asked quietly. "Mark you must be able to see something is going on here."

"Yes, I can see something is going on here. Two things in fact. I can see that my sister ran away in search of who knows what, and I can see that I didn't make myself clear enough when we last spoke of this.

"I will say it one more time so there can be no more misunderstandings. I want you to stop snooping into my family's business. Stop discussing this and put these ridiculous notions out of your head once and for all. You are going to be part of this family soon, and your loyalty needs to reflect that. You need to start acting like you still want to be part of the family. Am I making myself clear?"

"Mark," Justine started. She out her hand on Mark's arm. He shook it off angrily.

"Am I making myself clear?" he asked again, emphasising each word like he was talking to someone stupid.

"You've made yourself perfectly clear," Justine said. She stood up, tears springing from her eyes. She turned and ran towards the woods behind the square.

"Justine, wait," Mark called after her. He didn't know if she had heard him or not. He only knew she didn't look back.

* * *

AMITY SPOTTED Justine rushing towards the woods. She saw the tears streaming down her face. She excused herself from her conversation and followed Justine into the woods.

She found her sitting on a rock, looking out over a small stream, her knees pulled up to her chest, her arms wrapped around them.

Silently, she went and sat beside Justine.

"What happened?" she asked after a moment of silence.

Justine turned to her. "I think Mark and I just broke up," she said finally.

"What? Why?"

Justine told Amity how her and Mark had been ok, and then she told her about Sarah. About all what she had said and about Mark over hearing them. She told her what Mark had said after Sarah left.

"Oh Justine, I'm so sorry," Amity said as she pulled her friend into a hug. The friends hugged for a minute then broke apart, both of them looking out over the stream lost in their own thoughts.

After a moment or two, Justine broke the silence.

"I never imagined I'd be in a position where I had to choose between true love and doing the right thing. I always imagined they would go hand-in-hand."

Amity nodded. She had always believed the same. "Justine, I know you won't want to hear this, but can you not just let this whole Anna thing go? You've done your best. You've brought it to Mark's attention. If he thinks it's nothing, then maybe it really is just exactly as Anna's father said it is. Maybe she decided she would leave after all when she couldn't get him to change his mind. Or maybe it isn't that, but either way, it's not your problem anymore."

Justine shook her head sadly. "No, I can't just pretend this isn't happening."

She sniffed loudly and wiped her eyes, her mind made up. "I have to do what's right. It's all I've ever believed in.

I will just have to hope that Mark comes to see that I'm only doing what I feel is right, and that I'm not purposely trying to hurt him or his father."

"And if he doesn't?"

Justine swallowed, pushing down the new batch of tears which threatened to spill from her eyes at any second. "Then I guess I will have to do this alone," she said.

"What are you going to do?" asked Amity.

"I'm not sure yet," Justine said, "but I'll think of something."

CHAPTER 5

Mark sat alone on the back porch of the house. It wasn't overly late, but his father was already in bed. He had an early start in the morning.

Mark stared into the darkness. He felt like his heart was breaking, but he had had to tell Justine to stop poking into this. She was making his father out to be some sort of monster and Mark wouldn't allow it. His father had done everything he could to be a good father and a good role model, and to let Justine say those things about him made Mark feel like he was betraying him.

As he sat staring into space, his mind whirling with a hundred different thoughts, he heard footsteps approaching. He looked up to see Eli.

"Are you ok?" Eli asked.

Mark nodded. He thought for a second then shook his head. He wasn't ok.

"May I?" Eli asked, indicating the step beside Mark. Mark nodded and Eli sat down.

"What happened at the gathering today? I saw Justine go off into the woods and then I saw how angry you were. I wanted to come and talk to you then, but my father had things he needed me to take care of. I've just gotten finished."

Mark told him what he had overheard Sarah saying, and that Justine had made no effort to defend his family.

"I feel like she's judging us all Eli, that she think's my father and I are bad people. I know she hasn't mentioned me, but if she thinks that of my father, then how can I stay with her?"

"Do you love her?"

"More than anything in the world," Mark confirmed.

"Then that's how you can stay with her," Eli said. "Mark, she's not saying these things to hurt you or your father."

"Then why won't she just let it go?" Mark asked. "I've made my feelings about this clear."

Eli paused for a second as he worked out how to say what he needed to say.

"Have you ever considered that this isn't about you?"

Mark looked at him questioningly.

"She obviously loves you, anyone can see that just by seeing the two of you together. For her to continue to pursue this when you've made it so clear you disapprove doesn't mean she's trying to hurt you, or that she doesn't respect you. It means she feels so strongly about this, that she feels she has to keep on with it despite your feelings on the subject."

"Does that make it better?" Mark asked.

"Yes," Eli said. "It means she needs to do what's right, or what she believes to be right, above everything else. I'm sure she'd like nothing more than to forget about this whole thing, move on and get her happily ever after. The fact that she can't do that speaks volumes about her character. She believes Anna is in danger. She is putting Anna's needs before her own. That is a sign of a strong faith and a good woman. Don't throw all of this away over a disagreement Mark."

Mark considered his words. They made sense, he had to admit.

"It's a bit more than a mere disagreement. I just can't get past the fact that she feels this way about my father," Mark said.

"Try," Eli said. "You have to try for both of your sakes."

Mark nodded sadly. "I will try. I see what you're saying. Justine is a good woman, she really is, and I just have to accept that she won't always do what I want her to do if she feels that she has a just cause to act on. Thanks Eli."

They stood and shook hands. Mark watched Eli walk down the path towards his house and went inside his own.

He climbed the stairs and used the bathroom. He knew Eli was right. Deep down, he had known it all along, he had just had to hear it out loud. He decided he would go to Justine the next day and apologise for the way he acted. He just had to hope it wasn't too late, that he could convince her he still loved her. And then he would have to try and convince her to at least be subtle when it came to her feelings about the whole Anna situation.

He left the bathroom and went towards his bedroom. He would sleep on it and think about it in the morning on a clear head he decided. He would be able to word it better then.

As his hand reached out to open his bedroom door, he heard a scratching noise. He stopped and listened. There is was again. It was coming from the attic.

He moved towards the hatch that opened into the attic. His father's bedroom door opened.

"What are you doing?" asked his father.

"There's a scratching noise coming from the attic. I think we must have rats up there. I'm going up to have a look around and maybe set some traps."

"No," said his father. "I'll do it tomorrow."

"It's ok, I'll do it now," Mark said. He reached his hand towards the hatch. His father gripped his arm tightly, pulling him away.

"I said no," he said in a firm voice. "Do not go up there, is that understood?"

Mark nodded, the surprise clear on his face, and his father finally released his arm. He went into his bedroom, closing the door behind him. He understood alright, and he knew what he had to do. With the decision made, he fell into a troubled sleep.

CHAPTER 6

Mark woke up early, to the sun streaming in. As he lay coming fully awake, the events of the previous day came flooding back to him.

Justine. The conversation he had overheard. Their argument which had ended with her walking away from him. The conversation with Eli. And the way his father had reacted when he had offered to remove the rats from the attic. The rats that he thought weren't rats.

He got out of bed and quickly got washed and dressed. He knew what he was going to do. He was going to go to Justine and make her see he was sorry, that he had been wrong. He would beg her forgiveness. He had a whole speech worked out.

His mind made up, he set off in the direction of her home. She would be leaving for work soon, and he hoped to catch her before she got there.

Mark reached Justine's house. He stood along the end of the road, mostly hidden behind the hedgerow. He stood in silence watching for her. He saw the front door open and heard Justine call good bye to her parents. She walked along the street towards him.

When she drew level with him, he stepped out into her path. He heard her sharp intake of breath, and her head flew up to look at him.

"Mark. What are you doing? You scared me half to death," she exclaimed.

He stood blocking her path, determined to have her hear him out.

"I'm sorry," he said. "Not just for scaring you. For everything. For not believing you. For not listening. For trying to forbid you to go against what you thought was right."

He stopped. He had had a whole speech planned out, but now he was here faced with her, his words got tangled, his thoughts lost. He had to hope she could forgive him.

"What happened?" Justine said.

He looked at her, frowning with puzzlement. Hadn't she heard what he had just said?

"What happened to make you change your mind?" she said again.

"More than one thing," Mark admitted. "I talked to Eli and he made me see I was being unreasonable. That you had to do what you thought was right. I instantly regretted the way I spoke to you. I really am sorry."

"It's ok," she finally said, her face breaking into a smile. "I hated having to go against your wishes."

"Justine, there's more," he said. "I think you're right about Anna being in danger. Last night, I heard scratching in the attic. My father came out of his bedroom as I was going up there to lay some rat traps. He told me not to go into the attic. It wasn't so much that he said that, it was the way he said it. He was so adamant. He held my arm so hard it bruised. I think he might have Anna up there. After what Sarah said, it all makes sense doesn't it? It would stop her disobeying him publicly and bringing dishonour on the family, and to say she left explains why no one is seeing her anymore. And no one goes looking for people who leave. It's the perfect cover up."

Justine's head was reeling. "Oh my goodness. Do you really think he has her up there?"

Mark nodded sadly. "I really do. My father will have left for work by now. I'm going up there to find her Justine. I just wanted to speak to you first. I had to tell you how sorry I am, and how much I love you."

"I love you too," Justine said. She turned back the way she had come. "Let's go."

"What do you mean?"

"I mean you're not doing this alone. I'm going with you."

"I don't know about this," Mark said.

Justine smiled. "I wasn't asking your permission."

Mark smiled too. "I'm not going to be able to talk you out of this am I?"

"Nope," she said.

He was relieved he didn't have to do this alone. More than that, he was relieved that she had forgiven him. Eli was right, she was a good woman.

Amish Investigation

CHAPTER 7

Mark and Justine reached Mark's house and went in.

"Won't you be missed at work?" Mark asked.

"Amity will cover for me," Justine said.

"Ok," Mark said. "Right, I'm going up there. You stay here and shout if you see anyone approaching."

Justine nodded her agreement.

Mark went up the stairs and to the hatch. He pulled the ladder down and climbed up into the attic. He pulled the cord in the centre and the bare bulb lit up, casting long shadows into every nook and cranny.

Mark brushed aside the cobwebs as he stepped into the attic. A quick glance told him Anna wasn't here. Had his father moved her because he knew Mark was onto him? He walked into the centre of the attic and looked around.

There were piles of boxes everywhere, but no sign that anyone had been in here in months. He looked behind him and saw his footprints outlined on the dusty floor. There were no other footprints.

As he looked around, he saw a small pile of rat droppings. Maybe it had only been rats he had heard. But then why would his father over react so much to him wanting to come up here.

As he pondered this, he heard Justine's frantic shout from below.

"Mark, he's coming. Your father. Hurry."

Mark ran to the ladder and ran down it. He reached the bottom just as the front door opened.

"Justine, what are you doing here? Shouldn't you be at work?"

"I got the day off," Justine said. "Mark and I were just going to pop out for a walk."

He glanced up and saw Mark closing the hatch.

"What do you think you're doing? I specifically told you not to go in there."

Mark walked down the stairs in silence. When he reached the bottom, he faced his father. Until he looked into his father's eyes, he had had no real idea of what he was going to say. On the spur of the moment, he decided to give his father a chance to put this right. He deserved that much. "Where is she?" he demanded.

"Where's who? What are you talking about? Why were you in the attic?"

"Where is she?" Mark said again. "Anna. I know you had her up there in the attic last night. And now she's gone. What have you done with her?"

Mark knew it wasn't entirely true. No one had been in the attic last night, but he had to know the truth about Anna, and of that meant lying then he would have to face the consequences.

"Mark, you're being ridiculous, why would I have Anna in the attic?" his father asked, his face confused.

"I don't know, to protect your reputation or whatever other twisted reason you have used to justify this. I want to know where my sister is right now." Mark's tone was dangerously low.

His father visibly sagged. "Come into the sitting room. Let's talk," he said. "I'll explain everything."

Mark and Justine exchanged a look.

"Please," his father said.

Mark turned and walked into the sitting room. Justine and his father followed. They sat down and he began.

"I didn't lie to you when I said Anna had left the village. That much is true. I did lie to you when I told you I didn't know why. I'm sorry, I should have told you the truth, but I know you and your sister are close, and I didn't want you to hate me."

"Why would I hate you? What happened?"

Mark's father took a deep breath. Justine was shocked to see there were tears in his eyes.

"Anna came to me and told me she loved a boy named Jacob. She wanted to marry him. I told her no. She would marry Amos. Everything was already arranged and to go back on it would make us look weak. We would be considered time wasters and our reputation in the village would be destroyed.

"We argued for a while. I tried to make her see sense, but she wouldn't accept it. In the end I told her in no uncertain terms that she would be marrying Amos. She told me she wouldn't. She would marry only for love. She said she would marry Jacob or no one.

"I said she would do as she was told. She said if I tried to force her to marry Amos, she would leave the village. I said I wasn't going to change my mind. I thought she was bluffing. When I got home from work that day she was gone. And I haven't seen or heard from her since."

He hung his head. Mark and Justine exchanged a look.

"Father, I understand," Mark finally said. "Anna should have accepted your decision. But at the same time, I can see her point. I know how I would have felt knowing how much I love Justine if you had told me I couldn't be with her. And I still don't understand why you didn't just tell me the truth. Did you not trust me to see the wisdom of your decision?"

"Knowing the wisdom of accepting something and actually accepting it are very different things son. I had already lost Anna. I couldn't risk losing you too. I understand what you are saying about love, I would have felt the same, but sometimes, we have to accept that God's plan for us may not be the same one we hoped to follow."

Mark hung his head. "I'm so sorry I accused you of locking Anna away."

His father seemed at a loss for words. "Forget it ever happened," he said eventually.

"Father, do you know where she is exactly? I'd like to go and talk to her, see if I can convince her to come back."

He shook his head sadly. "I have no idea."

Justine, who had remained silent up until this point spoke up. "I have some friends who left the village a while back. I'll contact them, maybe they'll know where Anna is. It makes sense she would have tried to find someone she knew."

"Thank you," Mark said to her. He then turned back to his father.

"I understand everything you've told me so far. I even sort of understand why you didn't tell me the truth, although I want you to know I wouldn't have blamed you. What I still can't understand though is why you over reacted so strongly to me wanting to go into the attic."

His father smiled sadly. "I was merely trying to protect you. I wanted to make sure you wouldn't go in there and look around. Did you notice all the boxes in there?"

Mark nodded.

"Those boxes contain all of your mother's things. When she died, I couldn't bear to just throw them away, but seeing them every day in their places as though she would just walk back into her life was too painful. I boxed everything up and put it up in the attic. I didn't want you to look in the boxes and get upset when you saw what was in there, that's all."

Mark looked down, ashamed of himself. "Father, I'm so sorry," he said again. "I can't believe I accused you of such a terrible thing. I can see now that you did everything you did in an effort to protect me, and I have repaid you by hurting you."

"Mark, look at me." He waited until Mark looked up. "With the circumstances being so unusual, I can understand why you were suspicious, especially after the way I reacted about the attic. I think we are both at fault. We should have just been honest with each other. Truce?"

Mark nodded. They stood up and embraced each other. When they parted, Mark turned to Justine.

"Can we go and talk to your friends now?"

"Of course," she said, also standing up.

CHAPTER 8

It had taken Justine and Mark the better part of an hour to walk into the nearest town.

"I need twenty cents for the phone," Justine told Mark. He dug around in his pocket and handed her a coin.

She put it in the phone and dialled a number.

"Hello?"

"Hi Karen, how are you?" Justine said.

"Justine, how good to hear from you," Karen exclaimed. "I'm fine. How are you?"

"I'm ok thanks. Karen, I need a favour."

"Let me guess. It's about Anna."

"How did you know?"

Karen laughed. "Anna told me what had happened, why she had left. She said she had managed to go through your notebook and get this number when she knew she might have to leave. She told me you were engaged to her brother. I figured knowing you it wouldn't be long until you came looking for her. Justine, she needs you. This life isn't for her."

"I know," Justine said. "Do you know where I can find her?"

"She wouldn't stay here. I ended up giving her the details of a local homeless shelter. She's still there, or she was up until yesterday. I've been keeping an eye on her."

"Thanks Karen."

Karen gave Justine the address and some brief directions and they said their good byes.

"Well?" Mark said when she turned back to him.

"She's at a homeless shelter, but it's about fifteen miles away from here."

"I'm glad my father gave us this money then," Mark said. "We'll get a cab."

"But isn't that against everything we believe in?"

Mark shrugged one shoulder. "Sometimes you have to break the rules for the greater good."

They flagged down a cab and Justine gave the driver the address.

"Are you two running away?" he asked.

"No," Justine answered bluntly.

"No offense love. I see a fair few of you people dressed like that. They're usually running away. What brings you here then?"

"My sister left and we're visiting her," Mark said.

Mark and Justine exchanged uncomfortable looks. They weren't used to someone asking them personal questions, people minded their own business at home.

The cab driver raised an eyebrow. He obviously knew the address was for a homeless shelter. He didn't comment though.

They drove the rest of the way in silence. When the cab pulled up, Mark paid the driver and they got out.

"Thanks," Mark said as he closed his door.

The cab pulled away and they turned to look at the place they had come to. Its shabby door stood half open and through the gap they could see people sitting around on grubby blankets, their clothes in rags.

"This isn't what I was expecting," Justine said.

"Me either," Mark said. "This is more like a squat than an actual homeless shelter. We have to convince her to come back with us Justine, we just have to. She can't stay here."

"I know. We will. Let me talk to her," Justine said giving his hand a reassuring squeeze.

He nodded once and they went inside. The smell of partially rotten food and unwashed bodies rushed to meet them. Justine put her hand over her mouth and nose, trying not to gag. Mark was right. There was no way they could leave Anna here. Justine made up her mind they wouldn't be leaving there without Anna.

They made their way deeper into the squat, both of them scanning the people to either side of the passageways looking for Anna. People peered back at them from over the top of dirty blankets, their mud streaked faces wrinkling in distrust. Some of them shrank back as though afraid they would be attacked. Some jeered and made insulting remarks. Most just watched them silently.

Just as they were reaching the end of the passageway, and Justine was starting to think Anna wasn't here, Mark grabbed her hand.

"There," he said nodding in the direction of a girl huddled in a torn sheet. Justine looked closer and to her horror, she saw the girl in sheet was indeed Anna.

Justine gave Mark's hand a tight squeeze and swallowed with an audible click.

"Ok," she half whispered. "Go wait outside. Let me talk to her."

"No way," Mark said. "You can talk to her alone outside. I'm not leaving you in here."

He looked around suspiciously as he spoke, but no one was paying them any attention now they had decided they probably weren't undercover cops.

"Please Mark, this might be our only chance. You have to trust me," Justine said, still holding his hand.

"It's not you I don't trust," Mark muttered. Then louder, he said, "ok, I'll be right outside if you need me."

He turned and walked away before he could change his mind. Justine's hand felt suddenly cold where his had been against it.

With a determined stride, Justine approached Anna.

"Anna," she said when she reached her. "Are you ok?"

"Justine?" Anna exclaimed. "Is it really you? What are you doing here?"

"It's really me," Justine said, sitting with her back against the wall beside Anna. "I've come to take you home."

"No," Anna shook her head quickly from side to side. "I won't go back there Justine. There's nothing there for me anymore."

Her voice broke on her last sentence and she started to cry. "I don't belong there now, and I don't belong here. I feel so alone."

Justine reached out and wrapped her arms around Anna, pulling her to her like a mother would a child.

"It's ok," she soothed, rubbing the girl's back. "Everything's ok now."

Anna pulled back. "No it isn't. Don't you see? Nothing will ever be ok again. You don't even know why I'm out here."

"Yes, I do," Justine told her gently. "Anna I know about Jacob. And I'm sorry it didn't work out for you, but you can't just run away."

"I thought he would come after me," Anna said. "I really thought he loved me."

Justine thought for a second. She could let Anna think he didn't love her. That would make convincing her to return easier. But it would be wrong. She couldn't lie to her, couldn't be the one to break her heart.

"Anna, no one knows where you are. Mark and I only found out an hour or so ago. All we knew was that you'd left. Jacob wouldn't have known where to look."

"You found me easily enough," Anna said.

"Yes, but as you know, I have contact numbers for people here."

Anna looked down. "I'm sorry for going through your notebook. I was desperate."

"It's ok. I'm not mad. No one is. We're just glad you're safe."

"I bet my father's mad," Anna said quietly.

"I think he's more sad than mad," Justine said. "He loves you Anna, and he wants you to come home."

Anna shook her head. "I can't Justine. He'll make me marry Amos. It wouldn't be fair to either of us. I can't imagine spending my life with someone I don't love, and I don't think he would want that either."

Justine thought for a second.

"You know something Anna, sometimes things don't work out as we'd hoped. Honestly, I wouldn't want to spend my life with someone I didn't love either. But maybe, over time, you will grow to love Amos. He's a nice young man."

"I know that, but he's not Jacob."

"Anna do you still believe in God?"

She nodded. "Of course."

"And do you believe that your life should honour that belief?"

Anna nodded again.

"Then consider this. Maybe this is God's plan for you. Maybe, although you can't see it now, this is for the best and will give you the life God wants you to have."

"Why would God forsake me Justine? Why would he want me to be so sad?"

"I don't think He does," Justine said thoughtfully, "His reasons aren't always clear straight away, but He has good reason to guide you down a certain path. Anna, as a woman of faith you know how it works. You have an obligation to honour your parent's wishes. If your father wishes you to marry Amos, even after you told him you would rather not, then he has to have a good reason."

Anna thought for a second. "You're right," she eventually conceded. "My head knows you're right, but my heart is screaming at me not to do this."

"The truth is Anna, sometimes you have to listen to your head, and just accept that your father knows what's best for you."

Anna sighed loudly. "I've really messed up haven't I?"

Justine smiled at her. "I don't know about that. You made a mistake, yes, but that's not the end of the world. It's not too late to put it right. Come home with Mark and I now. Talk to your father. Tell him that you're sorry and that you will honour his wishes. I'm sure he'll be so happy to see you back home that he'll forgive you."

Anna nodded wearily. "Ok. I miss the village life and the people there so much. It's awful here Justine. Everything's so loud, and people hurt each other and steal from each other. They made fun of me at first, but eventually they got tired of it. I don't want to have to spend any longer here. I wanted to come home after the first day, but I didn't think I'd be welcome back there, not after the way I left."

"The village is your home Anna. We're your people. You'll always be welcome there."

Justine stood up and reached a hand down to Anna. Anna took it and Justine helped her up.

Anna embraced Justine. "Thank you so much," she whispered.

Justine smiled. "Let's get you home," she said.

* * *

JUSTINE WAITED IMPATIENTLY for Mark to arrive at her house. She had spent the day working on her rug with Amity. She had told Amity everything. She was so distracted, thinking about Anna and how everything had turned out, that she had stuck her finger with her needle four times. She would have had a more productive day if she had sneaked off to see Mark earlier, but he was at work too.

Justine was lucky to have Amity with her. Amity had worked even harder than usual to make look like Justine had produced more than she had.

When Justine finally heard a knock at her door, she practically ran to open it. She pulled the door open and Mark came in, a light breeze blowing in with him.

Justine felt a rush of warmth when she looked at Mark. She felt a moment's sorrow for Anna. She knew what she had said was true. She did have a certain obligation to fulfil her father's wishes for her, but she would hate to have to marry someone else knowing how much she loved Mark. It must be so hard for Anna, but it was all part of the faith. Sometimes, things weren't easy, and their faith was tested. She hoped Anna had passed the test.

"How did it go?" she asked Mark. She was almost afraid of hearing his answer.

Mark's face broke into a huge grin, and Justine breathed a mental sigh of relief.

"Perfect," he said. "Anna and my father had a long talk. She apologised for leaving, and he forgave her instantly. He was so glad to have her home, there was never any question of him not forgiving her. There were a few tears and a lot of hugging.

"Then he sat her down and asked her why she was so against marrying Amos. She told him it wasn't anything against Amos, she wanted to marry for love.

"He explained to her that it was too late. Her hand in marriage had already been promised to Amos. He told her a man is only as good as his word, and he had given Amos's father his word that the marriage would go ahead. He told her Amos was a fine young man and he would make an excellent provider for her and their future children.

"Anna cried a bit more, but she didn't fight him on it. She accepted that he knew what was best for her. Justine, I don't know what you said to her, I don't need to know. All I know is that you got through to her and brought my sister home. Thank you."

"Any time," Justine said. "I'm just pleased she's home. I feel for her though. Can you imagine if my father had said I couldn't marry you, I had to marry someone else? I know your father is doing what he believes is right, and I would never question that, but I do feel sorry for Anna."

"Me too," Mark said, "but she has really matured. I think getting away and seeing how different things are outside of this life, and realising how good she has it here have done her the world of good. She has reached the point of quiet acceptance. I think she now truly understands what faith is, and I think in a year or so, she'll see that this was the right choice."

"I hope so," Justine said. "She's a lovely girl, and she'll make a good wife. She deserves to be happy."

CHAPTER 9

Three months later.

Justine took a deep breath to steady her nerves. She was marrying Mark, her true love today. She wasn't nervous about making the commitment to Mark, she wanted that more than anything. She was just nervous about so many eyes on her. She wasn't used to being the centre of attention.

Anna walked over to Justine and smiled. "You're glowing Justine, you look so happy."

Justine smiled back at her. "You too. I'm so happy we are getting to have a joint ceremony and share our special day."

"Me too," Anna beamed. Then her face turned serious. "I want you to know how much I appreciate everything you've done for me. I know it didn't turn out the way we expected, but we got there in the end."

Justine reached out and squeezed her hand. "Let's go and get married," she smiled.

The two women walked to the door and left Justine's sitting room. Neither of them looked back. They walked to the square where the villagers were gathered waiting to witness the double wedding.

Justine glanced up as they reached the edge of the square. She had never been happier than she was in that moment for both herself and for Anna.

She smiled at Mark. Soon he would be her husband.

She stole a glance at Anna, and saw her dreamy smile mirrored on Anna's face as she looked across to where Jacob waited for her.

"Thank you for giving me the words to make my father see the difference between love and obligation, and how only one of those things could make me happy," Anna said. "I think you were right about it being a test of my faith. By keeping my faith and accepting that my father knows what's best for me, I was able to find the words to explain to him how I felt about Jacob, and why I just couldn't imagine marrying for an obligation. I think that when I talked to him properly without the hysteria and the tantrums, he realised how serious I was about Jacob, and how strongly I felt about the whole thing. I think he had always wanted me to be happy, he just didn't see that I could never be happy with Amos. And once he did see, he fixed it for me Justine. And Amos's family accepted it well. They agreed that it would be unfair to their son to force him into a marriage where he would never be loved, and where his wife would always feel like a prisoner."

Justine smiled at Anna. It wasn't the outcome they had been expecting at all. Anna had gone to her father and told him she needed to make one last attempt at explaining her feelings to him. She had told him that if, at the end of the conversation, he still wanted her to marry Amos, she would do it without any hesitation. He had agreed to listen. It seemed they had a new found understand, and a more equal relationship.

Justine wasn't sure exactly what she said to him, but whatever it was, it had been enough to make her father allow her to marry Jacob, the man she loved. Her father really had known best, but it had taken Anna's growing maturity and strengthened faith to make him see the right path.

Justine and Anna exchanged one last smile and walked towards Mark and Jacob. Today was the first day of the rest of their lives, and Justine couldn't wait for hers to start.

BONUS - DRUG OF CHOICE

"Come back with my yarn, you little scamp!" Charity Shrock leapt up, her feet hitting the porch floor with a thud. The black and white collie pup quickly disappeared around the corner of the house, a string of pale yellow yarn trailing in its wake.

"Darn it, Pepper, I need that yarn for Sarah's baby blanket. I'll be lucky to get it done now by the time the baby gets here." Charity took off after the frisky pup, hiking up the skirt of the mid-calf length traditional Amish dress so she could pump her legs faster. Darn dog would have the ball of yarn filthy or torn into shreds by the time she caught him.

Charity raced around another corner then ran smack into a brick wall and bounced off, landing on her bottom.

At least it felt like a brick wall. She blinked her smoky gray eyes and realized she hadn't hit at a wall at all. Well, just a wall of brawny chest.

"Whoa, slow down, before you hurt me." Jacob Zook grinned down at her from where he towered above her, hands planted on trim hips. "You trying to run me down?"

Charity sat on the grass in the same awkward position she'd fallen; legs spread, deep blue dress and black apron riding well above her kneecaps, *kapp* knocked askew. The force of the collision shocked the breath out of her momentarily but it didn't stop her cheeks from turning flame red.

"Jacob Zook, what are you doing there in my way? I'm trying to catch that blame dog of Zeke's and get back the ball of yarn he stole from me."

Charity's brother Zeke and Jacob were best friends and had been for as long as Charity could remember. It wasn't unusual for Jake to be somewhere on the property but she certainly hadn't expected him to be right around that corner at that exact moment.

"Well, I've heard about women falling for guys but aren't you carrying things a bit too far? Blaming the poor dog for making you run into me." He tried to make his brown eyes firm but couldn't really hide their twinkle.

Charity tried to keep a stern face; she didn't want to laugh at his teasing comments, but finally a grin won out.

"Well, the least you can do is help me up." She stuck out her hand and he grasped it, effortlessly pulling her to her feet.

A sudden jolt of electricity seemed to zing through their touching palms, a shock with an almost visible spark and audible crackle.

"Wow, now you're trying to shock me to get my attention? Charity Shrock, whatever has come over you?" His mischievous grin made the dimple in his left cheek dance.

Charity really didn't know how to respond. Their families had spent a lot of time together over the years, almost as if the two were blended into one. Jake's sister Becky was Charity's best friend and their parents were close as well. Charity even worked for the Zook family, helping take care of the guest houses they had built on their property.

Jacob had always been a part of her life. He was there when she lost her first tooth, there when she fell out of the apple tree and broke her arm. He'd been like another brother to her all these years.

Yet in the last few months something had changed. Somehow that brotherly feeling was transforming into a different sensation. She wasn't quite sure how to qualify it yet and it made her nervous.

"I'd love to stand here and listen to you babble on, Jake, but I've got to find Pepper. I need that yarn."

Jake moved to the side so she could pass then fell into step beside her.

"I'll just come with in case you need any help wrestling the dangerous beast for your treasure."

"Jake Zook you are a funny man." Charity shook her head. "You know you're not a little boy anymore, right?"

"Some things from childhood we should never give up." His voice took on a serious tone. "Like imagination. It's okay to have fun even if you are grown up."

For some reason they stopped walking at that moment and turned and looked each other directly in the eyes, a small smile playing across each of their faces.

Yes, something about their relationship was definitely shifting, metamorphosing. She wasn't quite sure what it was yet…but she knew it was coming.

CHARITY WAS up with the sun the next morning, dressed and helping to serve breakfast to her family of eight. Actually, there were only seven present since sister Sarah was married and living with her husband Paul's family in the next town. Her parents, her brother Zeke, and three younger siblings gathered around the table to enjoy a hearty breakfast before they started their workday. *Maemm* was pregnant again, an unexpected blessing, but this late in life pregnancy had been hard on her and Charity did as much as she could to lighten the load.

Charity stood at the counter whipping up a dozen and a half eggs to scramble. Sausage sizzled in a huge cast iron skillet and biscuits baked in the oven.

"Hannah, make sure the butter and jelly are on the table." Her twelve year old sister hustled to do as requested and soon everyone was seated and devouring the food set before them. Charity couldn't help but smile as she watched her family eat. At least one thing was certain; she had some serious cooking skills.

As soon as breakfast was over the women worked together to put the kitchen to rights then Charity headed out for work. Since she was only going to the Zook farm right next door she normally just cut through the orchard, crossed the wooden bridge over Serenity Creek and came out on Zook property. Today she followed her usual pattern and arrived at the Zook house half an hour before breakfast was to be served.

The guests who stayed at Zook's bed and breakfast were welcome to join the family for a traditional Amish breakfast or they could opt out. This beautiful October morning they were being joined by guests from three of the duplexes. Only the occupants of one cabin had chosen not to eat with the group.

Charity carried trays of food to the big round tables where everyone ate and kept the coffee flowing. Today's guests included several children and Charity enjoyed answering their questions and listening to their tales of taking buggy rides and seeing cows milked.

Breakfast over, Charity worked alongside Becky and finished tidying up the kitchen then grabbed her cart of cleaning supplies and headed down the flagstone path toward the two duplexes that housed the guests. Check out was 11 am and she knew it was half past that now. All the guests should be gone and she could get the rooms cleaned without a hitch.

She finished cleaning the first three units then headed to the last. A black SUV was still parked in the drive.

Charity frowned, noting it was cabin B, the occupants who hadn't come to breakfast that morning.

Checkout time was over an hour ago. Why were they still here? She knew they hadn't requested to stay an additional day.

As she approached the cabin, the door of the unit flew open. Three men came stumbling out, one man with his arms draped over the shoulders of the men on either side of him. The middle man appeared completely out of it, his head listing drunkenly, sun glasses slid well down his nose. He was swarthy looking and a jagged scar zigzagged down his right cheek like a bolt of lightning.

Spotting her standing there on the path the men froze in position. The shorter guy with the slicked back black hair stared straight at her, a cold, suspicious look in his obsidian eyes. The other man, taller and skinnier, began to chatter.

"Well, hello there, dear. Sorry we're a little late vacating the room." He smiled an apologetic smile. "I'm afraid our friend here is under the weather. He's going through a bad divorce and thought he could forget his problems by drinking a little too much. Don't worry, though, we've got it under control. We'll be out of your way in a heartbeat."

Charity didn't speak, just nodded her assent and watched as the two men carried their friend toward the car. Wow, he was really out of it. His toes dragged through the gravel, leaving a trail in the stones. One man opened the back door and they literally poured the guy onto the bench seat. The short guy stayed and fastened the seatbelt for the apparently unconscious man and the taller guy hurried back into the cabin. He reemerged in a moment carrying their bags.

"Thank you for your patience, dear. I left you a nice tip on the dresser." He smiled ingratiatingly. "This is indeed a lovely place. We'll be certain to recommend it to our friends."

Charity watched openmouthed as the tall, skinny man climbed behind the driver's wheel. In another moment they were gone, the SUV throwing up a rooster tail of dust as it traveled down the graveled path.

Charity shrugged her shoulders and turned towards the cabin. That was one thing she'd never understand about Englishers. Why did they think booze and drugs would make them happy? She guessed that was something she would never comprehend.

GO HERE TO READ NEXT CHAPTERS:

http://www.cleanstories.com/KADOC

Made in the USA
San Bernardino, CA
11 December 2019